Mother Walter and the
Pig Tragedy

Mother Walter and the Pig Tragedy

Mark Kramer

Alfred A. Knopf   New York   1972

THIS IS A BORZOI BOOK
PUBLISHED BY ALFRED A. KNOPF, INC.

Library of Congress Cataloging in Publication Data

Kramer, Mark, 1944-   Mother Walter and the pig tragedy.

1. Farm life—Massachusetts. I. Title.
S521.5.M4K7 1972   917.44'22   72-2252
ISBN 0-394-47954-8

Manufactured in the United States of America

FIRST EDITION

to Floyd Kendrick

Contents

Acknowledgments

The pieces in this book have appeared in somewhat the same form in the Cambridge *Phoenix*. Some of the proper names and personal information about various rural beings have been altered or are completely fictitious. I have done this to protect privacy, avoid trouble at home, and keep things legal. I hope that I haven't violated the spirit of authenticity by these occasional alterations and fabrications.

I would like to express thanks for the kind assistance of those who helped me with this book, especially to my parents. Others who were most generous include Harper Barnes, Ray Birdwhistell, Frederick Call, John Carey, Larry Gross, Stanley and Pauline Herzig, Jorunn Jacobsen, Bob Marvin, Clarence Miller, Jim Ord, Jeanne Rosenberg, Bill Schlansky, Bill Schreiber, and Sol Wirth.

Mother Walter and the
Pig Tragedy

Country Radicals

WHEN I FIRST MOVED to the wilds of western Massachusetts (east of Williams College and south of Mount Snow) my friend Ray warned me, "You better go back to New York if you don't want to go on a long strange trip, because living in the country will change you in ways you won't anticipate." My grandmother in Brooklyn offered much the same advice. "You don't need it. Who needs it?" she said, although she likes it well enough now.

Several years after ignoring both Ray and Grandma, I find they are both in some senses right. I've got troubles which would have amazed me if I'd been warned of them a few years in advance: my chickens never layed well; I've got to make more storm windows before snow sets in for good, and one corner of the barn needs jacking up. After years of same-old-troubles, new troubles like these feel refreshing. And what's more I've now got the sort of troubles I can share with friends.

I am amazed to enumerate the dozen or so good friends and neighbors out here who have retreated from bad old days as movement heavies. I don't mean just folks who used to stick their noses into an SDS meeting now and again, but former dedicated, fire-breathing full-time revolutionaries who, a few short years ago, would have sworn they were in it until death, and who expected to die young.

Though I was never in the "big leagues" traveled by some of my neighbors, my own move from the city was made more or less in retreat from activism. Nowadays it doesn't look much like retreat at all. Things are tough all over; out here satisfaction can actually be found now and then. The constant wearing frustration of movement life supplies its own peculiar gratifications too, of course, but it does not supply fresh trout.

Recently I've visited with some of my friends in the area who were formerly full-time urban guerrilla types. No, you don't find them nowadays reading the *County Blat* and cursing them damn pinko stoodents for foiling our noble President. More likely you'll find them writing books and movies, building a new barn, or squirming around half inside a clogged drainage conduit. Friends I've known since the time when they were ferocious disciples of this or that faction now breathe easy and greet me with a friendly, "Hi, have you folks dammed up that stream yet?" It's a little unreal.

Not that it's heaven on earth out here. If you'll pardon a moment's folk wisdom, you take yourself wherever you go. But things go slow enough here so that you can begin to feel what is really going on. Country radicals have not necessarily shed their analysis of, say, the power structure of the USA, or the nature of our electoral process. Nor are they necessarily on bad terms with old friends still active in the cities.

But they are certainly not into guerrilla mountain-fighting drills, or organizing farmers, or anything vaguely like that.

Something has changed for these people, and there are enough of them around so that I've wondered again and again what it is. I can come up with a rather long-winded explanation of it, but I cannot isolate one notion lost or gained.

Most movement whites I've known have been bright, middle class, and frequently affluent in their origins. They have been raised "morally," amid the trauma of the early sixties, and found out in late adolescence that the good guys weren't really the good guys and that *they* were the bad guys. Then they felt guilty, out of place, and without a future.

What's the point of being a teacher if the basic structure of public education corrupts and co-opts? What's the point of being a chemist when the only work is paid from defense contracts? A stockbroker? Advertising man? Never. The prospect of the future was (and still is) one of disenfranchisement. That leaves hundreds of thousands of liberally educated moral-as-hell students milling around, at the Pentagon, at the Democratic Convention of '68, at be-ins and Woodstocks, with a clear vision of everything that's wrong, and no place satisfying to go. (This says nothing of the masses of disenfranchised working class and black young people, whose oppression is far greater, and who do not have the same choices of straight careers open to them, let alone choices of alternate life-styles.)

There are many roads from this point, and only one leads to the country. People strike out on their own. Some retreat into scholarship, some declare the whole problem irrelevant by becoming artists, some "adjust" and pursue distasteful but orthodox occupations and tell themselves they are "different."

And some, naturally, immerse themselves in the movement. I do not think that the alienation suffered by white middle class students constitutes the sort of oppression which generates angry armies of the downtrodden. Middle class radicals, if they are committed enough, can cause fulfillment of their own prophecies by directly threatening the power structure, which will then directly oppress them and make them fighting mad.

But not many people will fight a revolution out of compassion. The oppressed student is, in a sense, only a haircut away from the bank president. Anytime he wants, the cops will treat him right and Dow Chemical will offer him a job.

Movement people will tell you that it is unsound to organize around "white liberal guilt" and that it is preferable to help people to see the nature of their own oppression. The question is complex: there's the draft, taxes for evil uses, rape of nature, drug laws, etc. But in terms of the quality of daily life in the seventies, the middle class student is not being robbed much by the ruling class, he is not beaten by the cops except at chosen times, he is not arbitrarily singled out for punishment, ordered here and there, separated from loved ones, or denied basic freedoms. Movement people are, however, subject to all these forms of oppression.

They are very wearing. They are blinding and make you see the whole earth as miserably ground under the foot of the dog-pig oppressor. They are also exciting, and help define the character in complimentary martyred terms. Political conditions are reprehensible and the movement allows alienated smart kids to throw their whole hearts and souls and intelligence into a struggle for just goals. For a time, it is exhilarating.

Eventually, some folks in the movement conclude they are spending too much time talking to themselves, or decide their efforts have made things worse, or grow frustrated that the miserable conditions, exhausting work, personal risk, and abuse they experience do not seem to be bringing revolution closer.

Some of them move to the country—which is the beginning of the story, not the end. It is suddenly possible to be engaged in interesting pursuits without suffering from zeal or paranoia. It is possible to be poor and live gracefully, to enjoy friends and lovers, to be in touch with the seasons and the society, to chat with factory workers and farmers without feeling the compulsion to proselytize.

The move to the country is a doomsday decision. It almost always starts out as a retreat, after other alternatives become too unpalatable. It would be nicer to change the world and make it a decent place. But after having a good whack at it, perhaps the best decision for some is to make the best of a bad lot. It turns out that a farm with friends is a very pleasant street corner to hang out on while waiting for the bomb to fall. Once you look for it, the sense of doom on New England communes seems pervasive.

There's trouble with the rural communities now and then—drug busts, enforcement of seldom-used sewage and zoning restrictions, midnight visits by gun-toting, beer-can hurling young bloods. But the woods dwellers persist because there is nowhere else as nice to go. They've tried school, careers, politics. Eachother is what makes sense, even though that doesn't make too much sense. It's great to have a home and great to feel competent.

If the country has changed me, it has done so by bringing life into clearer focus, allowing me time and room to see clearly what I am doing. And the consolation prizes we have out here make it possible to admit when we're losing ground.

Quite Contrary...
How Does
Your Garden Grow?

THERE SEEMS LITTLE REASON for anyone to eat poorly who has a half an acre of ground to till, a strong back, a calm mind, and a book or two about the experiences of older and wiser gardeners.

In fact, the gardening books that I have read, for want of enough to say, are finicky and over-particular about whether a seed should be an inch deep or two, and lead one to suppose that a rutabaga won't grow in the absence of "slightly sandy, but well-drained" earth.

This is not to say that books fail as a useful adjunct to a casual diligence. But if one takes them too seriously, he can go through the days of labor spent planting a garden feeling only dread of the results, and guilt that more care is not being taken. Lookit, you do what you can, and you will be surprised to find it more than enough.

A couple of years of experience watching the pole beans

climbing
poles, and watching
the potato bugs eating
the potato plants,
and you will know
what stuff in the
books to take seriously.
One thing to take with a
grain of salt is the suggestion that a mixture of salt
and flour, sprinkled on the leaves
of cabbage-family plants, will elimi-
nate worms. *The Organic Way to
Plant Protection*, which says many
useful things, also recommends this.
They say that the cabbage worms will eat the delicious
mixture, perhaps thinking it will make them fat and
healthy, and they will die as it solidifies inside them. A
cabbage worm is a beautiful chubby little fellow, exactly
cabbage green and about an inch long after a few days of
hard feasting on cabbages, broccoli, cauliflower, Brussels
sprouts, or kohlrabi. He is what he eats, and when killed
by crushing between thumb and forefinger (which accounts for most cabbage worm casualties in my garden),
gives off the odor of fresh coleslaw. He has been bred to
be a professional cabbage eater and doesn't have much
interest in salty hors d'oeuvres.

One day last summer, worried about the big holes
they were gnawing in my winter's food, I went after the
cabbage worms with a sugar shaker full of the deadly
salt and flour mixture. The next day it rained. The
bright morning after, the cabbage worms were back at
work, and the deadly mixture had hardened into a pastry
on the leaves, which soon baked a pale yellow in the sun.
With a bit of hand-picking I gained the upper hand over

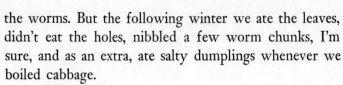

the worms. But the following winter we ate the leaves, didn't eat the holes, nibbled a few worm chunks, I'm sure, and as an extra, ate salty dumplings whenever we boiled cabbage.

Most of whatever you plant in a garden will come up. One year none of my New Zealand spinach appeared, but I think that was because it rained for six days right after planting, and the seed rotted in the ground.

There will always be some insects around, but they usually leave plenty, although I have lost a whole crop of potatoes to potato bugs. Gardening books recommend hand-picking into a pan of kerosene, but that seemed like a chore requiring too much diligence and patience, as they scatter off onto the ground as soon as the plant is given the slightest shaking. After a while I got desperate and used rotenone, an organically derived insecticide which is water-soluble and breaks down within a few days of its application. It worked and I saved a few plants. Most bugs aren't out to exterminate their supper, although those potato bugs seemed to be.

In the first weeks of June, flea beetles (which look like tiny beetles and jump like fleas) riddle the tomato seedlings with holes. By dashing wood ash onto each plant the beetles can be kept under control, and after celebrating the Fourth of July, they always seem to be gone for the season.

Some plants seem quite immune to insect damage. My celery and onions were actively avoided by hungry insects, and ladybugs lurking among the shady inner stalks of the celery starved to death waiting around to eat garden pests. Summer squash (yellow, crook-necked, and zucchini) grow fruit so fast that the bugs barely have time to hear news about where it is before it's ready to pick.

Most of the work in a garden occurs right at planting

time, which is traditionally on Memorial Day around here. I think the best way to till the soil for a garden is with a roto-tiller, which chops up and mixes the dirt as the operator walks behind it. (Lonely people should definitely write away expressing their desire to purchase roto-tillers, because the companies have a vast array of hokey brochures which they send out in a stream, once you start them off.) The tiller mixes "trash" mulch and stubble throughout the earth, where it rots quickly and increases the decomposed organic content of the soil. It also leaves the soil light and well aerated, which is good for earthworms and water absorption, both of which are great for gardens.

The trouble is that a good roto-tiller costs $300 or $400, and doesn't do anything but roto-till—it will also cultivate out weeds, if you space your rows properly, but one hoeing as seeds germinate and a heavy application of mulch after they sprout stifle weeds better and are better for the soil.

Most of the young people I know have instead spent $600 or $700 for some grumpy and ancient tractor with whose innards they become very familiar. It will also tow a work wagon, pull cars out of snowbanks, draw sawlogs out of the woods. It can be fitted with a snow plow, with a mowing machine, harrows, and haymaking equipment of all sorts. Also of great importance, it will most likely have a PTO or "Power take off," which is a powered shaft sticking out behind the transmission box, allowing one to run an endless belt to a portable saw rig —a great help in cutting winter wood.

Cousin Billy says to be sure and explain carefully what a plow does. It slices under and alongside a strip of sod or earth, and then as the tractor continues to move past the sliced strip, leads it back and over a beautifully curved sheet of metal (the moldboard) which turns the strip 180 degrees and lays it down adjacent to where it was to start with. The empty ditch left after the sod is rolled over is what is known as a furrow. It is not what you put the seeds into. The next strip of sod to be plowed flops into it, and the next strip after that flops into the newly formed furrow, and so on, until the only furrow left in a completely plowed garden (or field) is along one edge.

You can see that a plow does not mix turned-under grass into the soil, but buries it in a layer at the depth of the cut. It takes nitrogen and thriving and healthy soil bacteria to break down this sod, and when a worn-out piece of land is plowed up for a garden it will sometimes be several years before the sod rots completely and the soil benefits from its presence unless some nitrogen-rich substance is added.

After we plow the garden, we go around to the back of the barn and wrestle out a decrepit old sawtooth disk harrow—a contraption like a row of metal dinner plates on an axle which is dragged at an angle through the garden by the tractor to flatten the bumpy plowing and chew up any bits of sod which stick up. Perfectionists may follow harrowing by dragging a section of chain-link fence or a mess of old chains through the garden to make it smooth and good-looking. But I haven't found that the tomatoes notice details like that, so I stifle my compulsiveness and try not to notice it either.

The first year for a garden is the hardest, not just because you may not be sure of what you are doing, but because of purely physical problems with the soil. The rotting sod will take up nitrogen which would otherwise be turned into onions or green peppers. Witchgrass, red clover, and other hardy grasses will turn around and push for the surface again, and will even make inroads against thickly applied mulch (leaves or old hay, black plastic, or even newspapers laid between rows of plants to keep weeds from growing).

In subsequent years, plowing and harrowing get simpler, and the soil gets richer as all the mulch and old sod rots, manure and compost add goodness, and tilling lightens the earth. Insect and bacterial pests tend to accumulate over the years, but so do their enemies, and as plants grow stronger on the improving soil, they will resist disease better, and be more able to spare a few leaves for some hungry grasshopper.

A round planting time, seedlings appear in supermarkets and fruit stands: broccoli, tomato plants a hand high, and even young eggplants (you have to ask, and the boss's son brings them from the back room). If you wait a week or two, the price of a dozen plants might fall by half, and the plants are none the worse for having spent an extra fortnight in the greenhouse. We start many of our own seedlings back in February or March when it makes summer feel nearer than it really is. By the end of the first week in June friends will have appeared from other farms in the area, offering a leftover flat of pretty young Brussels sprouts, and perhaps accepting a dozen young cherry tomato plants in return.

Once we start to plant in the garden, the seedlings always get set out first, so that we can feel the garden is doing something even as we labor in it. Corn goes in a patch so it can cross-pollinate; different species of tomatoes go at far corners of the garden so they can't

cross-pollinate, and a few tomatoes are spared for the
top of the asparagus bed, for they are reputed to do each
other good. Nasturtiums, garlic, onions get scattered everywhere because some insects object to them. Then,
working with strings and posts to keep the rows straight
(not hip, but it makes hoeing and mulching much
easier), in go carrots. They take a whole two weeks to

germinate. We plant radishes on top of them to mark the
rows so we can avoid walking on the youngsters. In a
month the radishes get eaten, and the carrots need thin-
ning. Carrot seeds are followed by lettuce, chicory,
parsnips, salsify, turnips, beets, sweet corn, rutabagas,
spinach, beans (nice to see as they climb high pole
tripods set up for them), edible pod peas, chard, and a

few experimental rows of endive, leek, and black Spanish winter radish. As the setting sun glistens from the tubas of the Memorial Day band, we are just finishing off with hills of summer and winter squash, cucumber, canteloupe, and pumpkin.

A week later everything is up but the carrots and the salsify, which was planted from year-old seed and probably won't come up at all. It's time to mulch, time to stake the tomatoes so they won't get bad spots from resting on the ground, time to put up chicken wire around the garden to keep out the woodchucks (what few survive the terrible fury of Walter the dog), rabbits, and skunks.

It's not all sacred work. It's the worst time of year for bugs—mayflies swarm about and bite, mosquitoes are newly hatched and hungry, and black flies circle one's head persistently. The adventure which marked the garden's virgin planting no longer moves me much. Now it's the food I want, the good, fresh, healthy vegetables which taste real fine, the beans which don't need scrubbing before they're eaten, and the cucumbers which don't have to be peeled because they are not coated with oily wax to make them shine in the market and to increase their shelf life, the carrots, parsnips, cabbage, squash, beets, and rutabagas which will keep in bins in the cool cellar clear through until spring.

So the enjoyment is not really like the result of doing some real nice thing, like playing music or making love. It comes from the awful state of the world in general at least as much as it does from the nifty state of things on the farm. If vegetables like ours were available cheaply, we would be less apt to grow them.

Me, I'd rather be a good lawyer, but a good lawyer is of necessity a martyr this year. I'd rather be a good teacher, but a good teacher is one who struggles until he is ejected by the bureaucracy this year. I spent some years in that sort of struggle; I have only admiration for this year's good lawyers and good teachers, and it's nice here on the hill too.

Mother Walter
and the Pig Tragedy

BACKWOODS NEW ENGLANDERS have been celebrated for a hundred years for their reticence and brevity of speech. In vaudeville jokes, the wry, dry old codger always dumbfounded the city slicker with his clipped answers, as in, "Farmer, which way does this road run?"—"Ain't run noplace yet."

The reticence has another side as well, as I found out last winter at the height of a snowstorm. I asked my ancient neighbors if I could get them anything while I braved the storm to go to market. Old Mrs. Gurney answered with a single peculiar turn of phrase, "Not that I know of." It was humility speaking. I must have been right in thinking she needed something—only her foolishness kept her from remembering just what she needed. At least maybe that's how she meant it. Besides, I'm sure she had plenty of food laid in, being how this was their forty-third winter on the mountain.

The next time I ran into that humble reticence, I had a weather eye out for it and wasn't long fooled. I'd been thinking of raising some meat. Cows are a long-term project—about two years from birth until one is "finished off" and ready for slaughter. Then, you get perhaps six hundred pounds of beef for about twenty cents a pound. But you might starve waiting. Chickens are probably the most efficient converters of grain into meat in terms of pounds of grain for pounds of stew. But with chickens it's kill, kill, kill because they're barely a single meal and the whole of it not very pleasant. So the solution seemed to be a pig.

A few enterprising farmers around here keep brood sows. Bred to a boar at the right time, they yield up huge litters (ten to fifteen piglets late in February) which can be weaned and sold for up to $20 apiece as soon as the snow melts at the end of April. Many folks around here will raise them until late fall, then slaughter them for about two hundred pounds of winter meat. Most do their own butchering, and the old ways of preserving— canning, pickling, drying, salt curing, and smoking—are not lost, although the deep freezer is making them less common.

Armed with the intelligence that a pig will provide the most meat in the least time, I went on down to Floyd Kendrick's place to ask him how to do it. After the customary chat about the wetness of the spring and the expected denials that Floyd's arthritis was bothering him much, and the accepting of a steaming mug of heavy brown coffee, we got down to business.

"Floyd, I want to raise a pig."

"A pig, huh?" said Floyd. "A pig. Well, I guess that's a good idea, Mark. A pig."

Now I can't give you the whole feel of what went on here because part of it is in the accent, a slow, melodious, and contagious speech, a sound like a Boston short-order cook imitating Prince Phillip. It has an ancient and

friendly cadence, and survives only in those too old or too busy to have fallen prey to TV English.

"Well don't you think a pig's a good idea, Floyd?"

"Yes, yes. I raised some myself, though that ain't saying much."

I had talked with Floyd Kendrick enough to know when he has something on his mind. The conversation stands still. He would never come out and contradict anybody. But he simply wouldn't move on to a new topic until somehow he'd settled what was on his mind. So I asked him how he would go about it. He issued customary disclaimers about not being an expert, but just a poor old fellow who never amounted to much or else he wouldn't be here talking now "in this poor place," gesturing around his perfectly fine farm by way of apology. Then he came out with it.

"Now lookit. Suppose I'm a pig." I started to say something but he stopped me. "No, I'm not really a pig. I mean just fancy. Right? Now I'm out there in the pigpen all alone and it's the middle of July and I sees you coming out and you're carrying the bucket of slops for me and I says to myself, 'Oh. Here comes that fellow with that bucket of slops for me. Well, I might have some now and I might wait a while before I dig in. And I might eat it all, and then agin, I might just leave some.'"

I began to see the point.

"Now say I'm that same pig all over. But this time, there's another one in there with me. So I sees you coming with the bucket, and I says to myself, 'Here comes that fellow with the bucket. I better get right over there so's I can eat it all right off, before that other pig gets any.' That's the point, Mark. A pig's a hog—that's why they call him that. One pig alone won't amount to much. But you raise two pigs, two pigs and they'll each be so afraid of how the other's gonna get all the slops that they'll both eat themselves fat."

So it was two pigs. He also had a fine idea for how to keep them. One of the big problems raising any farm animal is keeping their quarters free of manure. Cows don't notice and would just as soon lie in it as on clean straw. As a matter of fact, dairy farmers clip and vacuum their cows with special vacuum cleaners. Chickens are alien creatures and I don't know how they feel about anything even though we sometimes keep some. Rabbits will make a toilet at one end of their pens and live at the other, given the chance. Pigs seem to have that inclination, but they give up easily and can seemingly tolerate far more filth than any other animal without getting sick. In olden days, thrifty farmers used to sometimes keep them in the manure pit under the work horses, and they would have a second go at the oats.

What Floyd suggested was a pig sled. "You cut some green poles, about twenty feet long and four inches wide, and use them as runners for a fenced-in pen on skids. That way, whenever the pigs foul their pen and root it all up, you just hitch the tractor to it, and draw it forward. The used part has been fertilized by the pigs and can be reseeded to good hay for next year. And far down the route the sled is going to take, you can plant some root vegetable to fatten the pigs later in the summer when the sled has been drawn down that far—turnips, rutabagas, carrots, parsnips, even some corn they can knock down."

The next day Floyd struggled into my car and we drove off to find some pigs. We made two visits, one to a cut-rate dealer who maltreats poor stock, and then another to an honest trader who commands a fair price. Floyd looked over thirty or forty sucklings, chose two he thought likely to fatten well, and we stuffed them in sacks and drove off. "You can tell they were feeding well because the tails on them two was curled, like a corkscrew. You see a sad pig and his tail will hang limp as a rag."

I threw them in the pen and dumped in a pail of vegetables—outer leaves and rotten fruits from a nearby road stand. I fed them day after day and it's like George Orwell says, they're very smart. They figured my feeding routine right away and watched me with great awareness, something cows and horses can't manage.

I wasn't going to name them, for fear that I'd grow too attached to do them in in the fall. I had visions of two 800 pound pet pigs riding around in the car with me. I grew attached to them anyway, so I named them Victoria and Albert. That way next winter I would be able to call the freezer the Victoria and Albert Museum. A month passed, and they grew shapely and gross with incredible speed, and crowded each other for choice morsels, as promised.

Meanwhile, under the porch, Walter the celebrated Manchester Guardian was nursing eight pups. And about the third week of nursing, just before weaning them, ferociously hungry from the task of feeding twice her own weight in dog, Walter received a visit from Aaron the killer hound down the road. And while we were off across the road, Walter and Aaron tore into the pigs, wounding them terribly.

We heard the screeching and the barking and ran to find Victoria and Albert at death's door, and Walter, still bloody, skulking in the far corner of the pigpen, her ears folded back flat against her skull. I ran off to fetch Floyd who left weeding his cabbages and rushed to penside. "The male, he might make it and he might not. The girl, she don't look none too rugged right now."

There actually is a last breath, after which there are no more, and I saw them both draw their last. Feeling numb and upset, we bled and gutted them. I was not up to the butchering, and was relieved by my friend Rex who not only can butcher, but also can repair a slate roof and build a house.

The next day we had a grand feast, with local lawyers, farmers' daughters, and many a freak from forty miles around. Floyd declined to come, saying, "You don't need no old fellow around." Everybody had a fine old time, nevertheless. Walter ate the bones with callous casualness—as if to say "Dogs will be dogs, you know." I felt cannibalistic. After all, I'd been on very intimate terms with my dinner. It was what you might call a moving experience, but after a few pensive hours I concluded that that's life.

Work

OF COURSE AT FIRST it was a thrill to drive a tractor around the barnyard and still more thrilling to be finally turned loose in the fields with a real job of plowing or disking to do. In fact, after years of fieldwork, driving the tractor is still a big pleasure.

Nevertheless, the advance past the "Lookatme, Ma" stage of farm work is one of those poignant upward passages in life—the soul grows firmer but only at great cost in innocence.

It seems impossible for a child of the middle class to work for long with his back and hands without feeling noble and exhilarated. Of course it's nice to feel that way even though "real" farmers don't seem to feel quite the same about it.

The exhilaration, however, is sometimes followed by a feeling that somehow the labor has been a game, that it need not have been performed this day, in this way, by me in particular; that it might as well have been hired out, or left undone, that I am on vacation and that some-day I will *really* get back to work and will sit down and write a book on Wallace Stevens, or make a real estate deal, or get it together to teach my neighbors the true nature of American imperialism.

The feeling that labor is an arbitrary pastime is a lead-ing cause of country failure. It's not that the work doesn't seem enjoyable, nor that it's too hard or too technically difficult (the know-how quickly becomes second nature). It's not even the lure of other more in-teresting or more profitable pursuits. It's the sheepish feeling that the toil doesn't count for much because it's not what one dreamed of doing at the age of twelve.

A former headmaster of Deerfield Academy observed

that, having elevated several generations from boyhood instruction to ruling class careers, he had found that a boy's character at twelve tells more about his eventual makeup than it does at seventeen. I think he said the teen years were "in parentheses."

City kids from well-to-do homes take inordinate pride in simple tasks everyone out here knows how to do. I'm sure the farmers who comprise my team of local advisors think I'm a fool for having to ask so many questions every time I want to plant a row of turnips or fix the carburetor on the chain saw. And of course city friends who come a-calling can't believe that I grew that big turnip or fixed that chain saw myself.

I tend to side with the city friends. I can't believe it either, at least not when I'm in a certain self-critical mood in which I apply the standards of my own twelfth year to my twenty-sixth.

I am visited at such times by myself as a stuffy little boy —and he'd soon have me back in graduate school, or editing books in Manhattan. Praise God, he isn't with me often, because it's grand to become completely absorbed in the ecstatic heave-ho of haying or the judicious tracing of a block in the truck's gas line.

The way I can keep him at bay is to avoid theorizing, to blush when accused of tilling the earth, ah the soil, and harumph when assured that hard work is good for me. I must remind myself now and then that if I feel sheepish about playing farmboy, I would feel far worse sitting on my can doing less pleasant work in order to pay someone else to have my fun—even if it might seem more proper to that stuffy twelve-year-old cretin inside me who would most of all like to join the Rotary Club.

So to hell with the sheepishness and to hell with the cretin kid. I heat my house with wood that I cut, draw in, split, stack, and stoke myself (the ashes end up adding sweetness to the garden), and I'm learning what it means to keep a body warm. That is, I know when I feel cold, and can trace the sunshine through trees and fire, into the winter air to warm my cold city heart.

Stand-in Milker

I'T'S A RARE TREAT for Hank to miss a milking—this past year he missed one a week or two after Thanksgiving when he went to see his brother-in-law in Maine. The time before that was when the Clabberville Comets, which is Hank's Little League team, won the championship and went to Boston to see the Red Sox.

Well, the Clabberville Comets did it again, knocking down the Burinton Bulls in an extra inning play-off thriller, and not too long ago Herman Paddington's new school bus pulled into the barnyard just after morning chores, loaded up with team and mothers and Hank, and drove off to the ball game. That left me to do the evening milking, which I always like fine, and I wish his team would win the championship twice a year.

Bruce from down the road, the one who raises beef cows, came up to feed the cows and calves, and cousin Billy came up from New York special for the occasion to carry the pails of milk. I learned to milk from Hank, who is a wonderful teacher. He never used to say, "Hey, how come you didn't feed out the rest of that bale of hay?" He'd say, "Do you think they should have a little more?" as if I was already an expert and he was the one needing advice. He coaches the same way, which is why the Comets keep winning the championship.

The day before the trip we had a dress rehearsal. It was six months since I last milked for Hank, and I had not kept up on the special problems of his herd—which cow is fighting mastitis in her front quarters, which one's udder hangs so low to the stable floor that she can only be milked with the small milking machine, and which one is just learning her place in the barn. Sissy had been trying to take another cow's stanchion when first let in from the day pasture. If I didn't get her into her own place in time, she would cause a chain reaction, leaving the barn a mess of milling animals, none in her right stanchion.

When they are where they belong, the cows stand in two straight lines, tail to tail, with an aisle down the middle and their heads stuck through stanchions, so they are gazing out the windows. The stanchions permit them freedom to lie down, move a bit, and feed on the hay and grain which are offered during the milking.

The stanchions keep the cows stationary enough so that their prolific production of manure falls pretty much in a gutter which runs along behind the cows. An automatic scraper then shoves the manure to the end of the barn and on out to a spreading machine, which later throws it every which way around the fields as it is dragged along behind a tractor. Since this system became common, in the early fifties, almost no one shovels much manure by hand anymore.

Once in a while you see a barn where the lines of cows face each other. This makes feeding easier, since one central aisle then gives access to everybody's mouth. With Hank's setup, though, milking is easier because one can move from milking a cow in one line to milking a cow in the other line without having to walk all the way to the end of the barn, around the line of stanchions.

Hank uses three milking machines that operate by vacuum piped around the barn from a pump in one corner. Between each pair of stanchions is one air spigot for attaching the machine. Cows that share a common air spigot cannot be milked at the same time. For this reason, a rather complicated order of milking is followed.

The night of the dress rehearsal, Hank went around the barn with a can of veterinary disinfectant, letting fly

a mist of purple dye to number the backside of each cow. The first three cows to get milkers were all labeled number one. The next three were sprayed with number two's—rather two of them were, but the third was all black on her butt so I promised to remember her. The order insures against trying to milk a cow twice or skipping one.

By the following night a rain shower had dribbled the dye down the flanks of most of the cows. Whitey, who was then the freshest cow of the herd, had a big notice scrawled on her side, "Calf Milk Here," meaning that we should feed some of Whitey's milk to the youngest calves being raised up to join the herd. The sign must have appeared a bit strange to passersby. I can just hear old Walt shaking his head and saying to his wife, "If I was a calf I'd have me a drink right now!"

Cousin Billy and Bruce and Betty (Hank's eleven-year-old daughter) fed out the grain pellets, which lure the cows to stick their heads through the open stanchions in the first place. I started up the milk cooler, assembled the milking machines, and we were ready for the cows.

Betty whistled up Lady the cow dog, opened the gate from the pasture, and set the dog to bringing them in.

It is a pleasure to watch a well-trained herd dog no matter how many times one has seen it. Hank stops whatever he is doing when Lady brings in the cows and comes to the window to watch her work. The dog flits back and forth around the whole rear perimeter of the mob of cows, nipping at their back heels and never leaving off irritating them until they are headed in the right direction and on the move.

Yet she can be brought to a halt with a single whistle, dropped flat with a high trilling sound, called in to goad more fiercely, or cautioned to ease off a bit. A pointed finger will send her up the steep climb to rouse up a dry cow, not used to coming down with the others, should Hank want to take a look at her. Once the cows are in, Lady must be tied up out back because "she always wants to work and she makes the cows nervous."

We made the cows nervous too, as is the case with all strangers coming into a barn where strict routine is usually followed. The milking went along easily, and as the cows were finished, their udders were dipped in antiseptic solution. The whole herd was again turned out to pasture an hour and a half after they first came in. But there was about a hundredweight less of milk in the bulk tank than had been there the previous night—about $6.50 profit lost for Hank.

Cows are conservative by disposition and are upset by any sort of change. If Hank leans his head into a cow's flank in a particular way while he's washing off the bag before milking, and I do it differently, the cow will worry about it, and she'll hold back some of her milk.

The washing of the bag tells the cow that the milking machine will be on her very soon. She then will "let down" her milk. A hormone, oxytocin, is released, which allows the milk to descend to the teats and flow freely. Studies have shown what every dairyman knows —that it is important to wait at least half a minute between washing and starting to milk, and it is even more important to get the milker on within about ninety seconds of washing. After that, the cow ceases to let down the milk easily, will give less for the day, and runs a great risk of contracting mastitis as a result of being kept waiting.

Cousin Billy was standing next to me while I washed off a cow and expounded upon the subject of cows letting down milk around strangers. Cousin Billy says, "So it's the truth!" and of course I say, "What is the truth?" and he says, "Classic novels always seem to apply to whatever else you are doing while you are reading them." Next thing you know, he has a copy of Thomas Hardy's *Tess of the D'Urbervilles* out of his back pocket and he's showing me a page:

"To my way of thinking," said the dairyman, rising suddenly from a cow he had just finished off, snatching up his three-legged stool in one hand and the pail in the other, and moving on to the next hard yielder in his vicinity, "to my thinking, the cows don't give down their milk today as usual . . ." "Tis because there's a new hand come among us," said Jonathan Kail.

When the last cow was up in the pasture drinking water from the old bathtub trough, Grandma came out with some cold beers for us and said, "Looks like you been working. But how would you like to have had all them cows to milk by hand?"

"I wouldn't keep so many," I said to Grandma.

Cousin Billy said, "But you don't keep any now."

A Thing or Two
About Cows

IF A COW WOULD—I know it won't—but if a cow
would look up and smile at you, do you know
what you'd see?

No top teeth.

Way in the back of the mouth where no
one ventures there are top molars for crushing
cud. But in front, where the business of tearing
grass is carried on, you'll find only broad chisel-edged
lower teeth. They press grass against a hard gum pad on
top whence the tender shoots are torn by a raising of the
head.

Let us never forget, as some dairymen have, the
nature of a cow. She started out as a wild animal, a herd
animal who lived on the edge of semitropical grassy
plains, alternatively taking to the woods and browsing in
the open. Cows have been bred and refined until little remains of the ancient beast. If modern dairy herds were
left to their own devices in some southern wilderness,

they might not survive, so much has been lost of their original instinct. They would graze and they would copulate. But perhaps they would be too delicate when calving or stricken with disease, since weak but productive animals have been propped up and helped along with sheltered lives and modern drugs for so many decades.

The calves especially would have a hard time. *Hoard's Dairyman* ($2 a year, Fort Atkinson, Wisconsin, the best and most informative farm magazine) said that, on the average, sixteen percent of a dairy herd will die while still calves, and that's with medicines, housing, and watchful care.

Some breeds have been so single-mindedly mated for high milk production characteristics that other factors, important to survival, have been lost completely. Holsteins, for example, which are the huge black and white cows most commonly seen in New England, cannot easily have their first calves by Holstein bulls. Traditionally, at about fourteen months a prospective mother is turned loose with a tiny scrub Angus bull and allowed to conceive. Why should a farmer give up his chance for a full-blooded replacement heifer (a female which can be raised to join the milking herd)? Because first-time Holstein mothers aren't big enough in the pelvis to admit passage of the large purebred calf. And rather than take the chance of losing a mother (worth, at that point, at least $350), the farmer will sell the half-breed calf for veal and content himself with getting the mother into production.

In recent years, some of the more innovative dairymen have been using purebred Holstein sires with first-calf heifers, after assuring themselves that the bulls yield small offspring.

Some herd characteristics have not been bred out of the animals however. They establish a strong pecking order. They will try as best they can to give birth in some secluded spot in the woods, jumping fences and fording streams in their efforts to find privacy. And they will act timid and bunch together when confronted with a threatening beast. A cow with a newborn calf can be dangerous, attacking dog or stranger. Also, at calving a cow will eat its placenta or afterbirth to hide from lurking predators any hint that a newborn calf is hidden nearby.

Christopher the anthropologist says that he saw a few half-wild cows in the interior of Brazil, who mostly fended for themselves and gave the Indians a trickle of milk now and then. But in the United States, the milk cow is man's creature, and his burden.

If a cow is to feel contented, she must be treated like a career soldier: she's happy when she knows her place in

LONG HORNED CATTLE

the herd, when she knows where she'll sleep and what her next meal will be, who will come calling and what noises and strange people are about. She will respond to any breaks in routine by lessened milk production.

For hundreds of years, the standard method of storing a cow has been the stanchion barn. In summer she might wander through miles of pasture (about an acre a cow of good grass, or ten of sparse woods) feeding herself. But come the first hard frost, she will be locked in the barn, her neck gripped in a stanchion, her tail pointed out over a gutter. There she may remain without a moment's freedom through five months of winter.

It is not as nasty as it sounds, owing to the nature of the cow. The temperament of the cow is so placid that the word which describes it has passed into general usage in the idiom "to have a bovine nature." The cow doesn't mind anything much as long as it is the same as it was yesterday. She will keep on slurping water and munching hay while she is injected, sprayed, shoved, washed, and milked.

The stanchion barn is quite convenient, and most farmers (though not most cows) still use it. The arrangement keeps the cow where she is the least trouble. Her waste (up to two hundred pounds a day) falls where it may easily be scraped or shoveled off into a cart or pile. It cannot foul her food. She is in place, ready to be milked, with no rounding up, and she may easily be observed for signs of illness.

As long as herds are smaller than thirty or fifty cows, the method is good enough. After that point, its disadvantages emerge. So, most large herds now have given up stanchion barns for other housing arrangements. Rather than bringing expensive plumbing, vacuum pump hoses for the milking machine and perhaps milk pipeline, to each stanchion, let the cows be free to eat from a central bin, drink from a central trough. Lead them to be milked at a central location, called a "milking parlor."

The innovation which makes "loose housing" possible is a stall attractive to cows wandering in a big barn, but which, by a clever arrangement of rails and overhead struts, forces the cow to lie down upon entering. This prevents her from fouling her nest. The only decent place for the cow to leave manure is in a wide central walkway, easily scraped by a small tractor or electric barn cleaner.

The cows learn when milking time comes and line up, frequently in nearly the same order day after day. They are admitted, commonly four at a time, to sets of tight stalls on each side of a waist-deep working well where the milker can conveniently reach the udders. As one group of four finishes, the milker switches the machines one by one to the four cows on the other side of the pit, then releases the first four, and accepts four new cows. By this technique one man can milk nearly twice as many cows (up to sixty an hour) as he could moving from animal to animal in a stanchion barn. The only major loss in the free stall and parlor system is some degree of individual attention to each cow. But a daily inspection of the herd by a sharp-eyed herdsman will help offset this loss.

The advent of the new system for milking has revolutionized dairying. There are not many yet, but some "milk factories" now keep up to four thousand cows at one facility, milking around the clock in parlors holding forty or sixty cows at once, and feeding entirely bulk hay and grain brought from elsewhere. More typically, a farmer might switch from stanchion to parlor and increase his herd size from fifty to a hundred cows. This puts pressure on his neighbor down the road who is still using high labor methods to tend half as many cows, working just as hard but unable to invest the capital to expand.

As this goes on, farms move with the rest of our society. The little man disappears, wealth consolidates, the big operators grow bigger, and the animals who are the cause of it all move further and further from the beast.

Leaving the Farm

THERE AREN'T MANY JOBS left now about which one can say that work and spirit grow with each other. Medicine must be one of the few—especially as it is practiced by many conscientious young doctors coming out of medical school in the past few years. Farming is another—at least as it has been practiced up until the past few years.

Maybe I am mistaken about this whole notion. More likely, in every job, work and spirit grow together. It's just that in modern U.S. culture the jobs are often meaningless, foolish, innocuous, destructive, or even treacherous, and the spirit grows accordingly. That is why I am so sad that my friend Hank must sell his farm.

After three years of wavering, he is getting out. The real estate broker has already been in, and Hank has signed a contract.

What does the broker see? An 1810 brick farmhouse with four chimneys and many bedrooms, partially modernized (central heat, but the wood stove helps on cold days). A thirty-stall stanchion barn with concrete floor, sound and not over twenty-five years old. Other sheds and buildings too numerous to mention. The house, completely surrounded by its own land—ninety-six acres of it, much of that in steep pasture or woodlot, also including a flat field of three acres across the road from the house and fronting on a small river, and several other fields, all in excellent condition. The house site a bit too close to the road—though it is not a busy road—for the tastes of the more modern buyers. Asking price? Say $67,500.

What does Hank see? He sees men who make a third again as much as he by doing factory labor eight hours a day. He sees the sale cost coming into his pocket, and a lesser amount going toward the purchase of a small house. He sees his boys going off to learn how to be coaches in small-town high schools, for they are both stars of their school teams. They won't be farmers. They don't like the work, although now that they are older, they do it with little fuss. He sees an end to the incredibly long hours—up at five and, summers, keeping up the pace until nine at night. He can survive doing custom farm work and helping city folk fix up their summer homes.

He is waiting for a buyer. He's in no hurry and can happily wait a year or two until he gets his price. So he's still out there every day, farming like there was no tomorrow, as if his property is not among the broker's listings. The other morning he had just finished plowing the nine or ten acres he puts into feed corn for winter silage and had turned to picking rocks out of the fields—not the little potato-sized ones gardeners painstakingly remove, but fifty-pound boulders which the frost heaves up from far below, half a dozen new visitors to the acre after each winter.

I ambled across the field to have a word with Hank, all the while sniffing the fresh-turned dirt, looking through squinted eyes past the sun, scratching a fresh mosquito bite, shooing away a cloud of mayflies, and otherwise appreciating spring.

"I'm going blind, Mark," he announced as I came within earshot.

"What!"

"No, not really. Didn't you ever hear that one about rock picking? Old-timer says when you first start a field there's a rock to pick every ten feet. By the end you're so blind you're lucky if you can see the big ones."

Thirty cows, thriftily and intelligently managed, barely support Hank's family. The operation requires constant coordination. It's quite a trick to judge when to do each of the thousand pressing tasks—when to spread manure in order to be done in time to plow, while not starting so early that the tractor will get bogged down in muck and take half a day to dig out.

Coordination of accounts is an equally exacting chore, a constant robbing of Peter to pay Paul, all the while keeping Peter happy. When does the milk check come in? When does the check from the calf auction (where the first calves are sent, when mother Holstein is bred to a scrub Angus to produce a small, supposedly safer-to-bear child) come in? Will the money cover the grain bill for this week? Producing cows need many pounds of costly high-protein grain and food supplement every day —no grain, no high milk production; no high milk production, no farm. But the grain man has to be paid.

How to get grain cheaper? Buy bulk instead of bagged grain. But there has to be a place to store it—a grain room on the upper floor of the barn which will unload downstairs by means of a chute. No money to build grain storage? Feed grain and use those big milk checks to build it . . . In about ten years the lower grain costs will offset the cost of the storage room, and from there on, the room is straight profit.

For a while Hank thought of expanding, suddenly and drastically, of building his herd to twice its size and switching over from stanchion milking to free stall and parlor. It is hardly surprising that he faced this dilemma. Every man milking thirty cows has experienced it in recent years. He would have had to borrow $35,000 to do it, and it would have committed him once and for all to spend the rest of his life farming. With twice the milk check coming in, could he have had more time to put his feet up in the evening, or to coach Little League? Would modernizing and doubling his stock have given him more spare time? Probably not a single second more.

With a fancy new setup it would have taken him a bit over an hour to milk sixty cows, as it now takes him a bit over an hour to milk thirty. He would have had twice as much corn to grow—twice as much manure spreading, liming, fertilizing, harrowing, planting, cultivating, cutting, chopping, and storing in silos. He would have had twice as much hay to get in, twice as many sick animals to watch, births to keep an eye on, calves to bring through such childhood ailments as all calves contract. And sixty cows are still not enough to justify hiring a hand to help, except during occasional peak season crises.

Thirty-five thousand dollars debt, plus interest, pays for expansion. Expansion, over the course of fifteen or twenty years, might pay back the debt.

Farming is about the only business I can think of where supplies are bought retail and produce is sold wholesale. Every year, the work gets no easier and the financial burdens grow heavier because inflation has raised the price of feed and equipment while government controls and the contracting milk market have kept milk prices relatively stable. No available road for expanding his operation would alter the prospect of continuing debt, continuing fourteen-hour days, and continuing want of leisure.

"If I'd have been ten or fifteen years younger and in the same situation, I'd have plunged in and stuck it out." Hank is not yet forty, but by the time the debt could be paid and the larger farm would have started paying a larger return, he would be nearing sixty. During the summer now he works too hard to be in peak condition. His hernia troubles him, last year he thought maybe he had an ulcer, and working to bring in four or five hundred bales of hay while the sky blackens and a storm moves in, he occasionally feels a dizzy spell from sheer nervousness.

Hank has taken a few vacations in recent years, but none longer than two days, because he must get someone else in to do the milking. While a stranger (usually me) can do well enough for a few days, there is always the risk of losing a cow suddenly to illness or a difficult calving if it is not watched closely by someone who is familiar not only with dairy farming but with the particular herd.

Hank's wife faces the same sort of daily grind. Though one would hardly think of Jo-Anne as a liberated woman—she cooks all the meals, sews and washes, shops and keeps house—she shares in all the decisions about the farm. She keeps the books and plans the strategy for making ends meet, and is the one to say no new tractor, make the old one last. She shares milking chores and drives the truck during haying and corn cutting. Frequently the youngest boy is not in his mother's arms, but riding on his father's knee while papa drives the tractor. Hank says, "The thing I think I'll miss the most is riding tractor cultivating corn at maybe six in the morning with little Benjie on my knee, and nobody else in the family even well clear of their beds yet."

Jo-Anne was, I think, the one who kept the most realistic perspective during the years Hank was unsure about whether to expand or get out. She understood that the compensations in farm life might make it worthwhile for her husband to stay in, even at the cost of hard work and little spare cash. After all, no other walk of life open to him here allows him the same range of skilled activity, nor demands even a small part of his great knowledge of animals, crops, weather, fences, cattle dealers, the moods of machines, plumbing, and the neighbors. But she was never enticed by the thought of going "big-time," of having a setup like you read about in *Farm Journal*. She knew the cost, not only in dollars but in spent nerves and

FARMER SNUG'S RESIDENCE DURING HIS LIFE TIME

spent health, of running a farm that carries a big debt, and she made her opinions known to Hank. I think she brought him down to earth.

The old order is dying, the rural social order with roots which stretch back clear to medieval England. Farmers whose great-grandfathers were farmers now must become handymen on city people's summer estates. There is no way out of it. I know of three farmers in town who have closed out in the past half-year. It is romantic to wish they would stay in business. Only a fortunate few farmers can possibly keep at it—ones who have had the opportunity to buy adjoining farms cheaply, whose land is the richest in the county, whose sons are interested in sharing the farm, whose fathers left them the capital to expand without overextending themselves. For the rest, only a tenacious New England fortitude has kept them in even this long.

THE SAME PLACE UNDER FARMER SLACK'S MANAGEMENT

The old order is dying, and I find myself close in next to the victim, listening for its last gasps of wisdom, watching for telltale signs of vitality which might upset the morbid diagnosis. There was a time when I would have zealously explained to all comers about alienated labor, the dehumanization inherent in capitalism, the concentration of capital in fewer hands, the vice of economic planning to benefit corporate and not communal interest. Such thoughts occur to me still. It's just that next year will probably not be the year the banks fail, the workers unite, and Hank's farm is returned, along with a medal, to the people, in trust of its rightful guardian.

So I am left feeling indignant toward the bankers whose interest rates rule out Hank's installing a milking parlor, and I am left with the suspicion that that analysis is, at the moment and for me, of no practical use. I am left with another feeling, more frustrating because it is not hitched to any suggestion of righteous actions: I think "it's a shame" that events are working out this way. I dread things to come soon, when the area I live in goes the way of southern Vermont, the relics of its "atmosphere" peddled for export to the city, its honest citizens either moved out or converted into dishonest servants of city folk at play.

Hank's relatives were farming the same place one hundred and twenty-five years ago, and this town has been, until this decade, almost exclusively agricultural. This *is* the time that things are changing for the worse. Hank's knowledge, learned helping his father and grandfather while he was growing up, is not available any other way. I read a couple of studies of when hay is best cut—when it "has the most milk in it," but I still didn't know anything useful about it until Hank repeatedly pointed and said, "That's what they mean when they say it's gone too woody," or, "That's beautiful stuff. Too bad I won't have time to cut it for another three days," or "Taste this shoot. You can see why cows like it." He had read the same studies, but I'm sure he learned more from remembering what his cows ate and how much milk they gave out afterwards.

I feel uncomfortable merely feeling that "it's a shame." Hank will end up better off financially, more at his ease, perhaps happier, and it's no shame at all that these good things come his way. I suppose part of what I consider a shame is the loss of opportunity to practice his craft. I admire the diversity and specificity of his knowledge, and the virtuosity he applies to the daily problems of running a farm. That is a city boy's admiration, I know, because men around here are supposed to know these things. Yet no factory job and no contract to mow another man's field can give constant play to Hank's knowledge. He has been forced by hard times in the nation's economy, and perhaps by the nature of that economy, to trade in independence for security, resourcefulness for efficiency. Hank's youngest son won't know his dad's craft, and he will be prey to the same modern work city boys are prey to, and to the same malevolent spirit.

Hank's departure is, of course, a product of his expectations. If he didn't want to raise a fine family, take them to church Sunday morning, and drink beer with the Knights of Columbus, things would be different. If he would only groove on raising enough food to feed his family, if Jo-Anne was only into weaving homespun and sewing far-out rags for little Benjie, everything would be fine. The sometimes absurd fashion of my own life here becomes all the clearer in the light of Hank's staunchness.

The young people who move to the country may be the only heirs to Hank's craft. But we do not practice the craft with the same style or intent. We are transplants with new roots, roots which don't go very deep, and which seem somewhat forced, even as far as they go. We have learned how to take care of ourselves, and we have developed a quick myth that we know how to take care of each other, and that we belong to some sort of community. It may be true, but of the eight or ten farms of young people around here, only one is a working farm with sufficient produce to sell to "our" community outside. One reason for this is economic. It takes a minimum of $5,000 to $7,000 capital just to grow ten acres of organic vegetables for the summer. You need a tractor with front-end loader, a truck, a manure spreader, cultivator, and a gang of friends with the will to put in long hours for low returns. Even after the produce is grown, there is no channel for marketing it on the East Coast, so one must vend it from store to store, or open one's own vegetable stand. It's all possible, just as it would be possible for Hank to struggle on, assume larger debts, and keep doing what he was doing. But the life that would be best for him, like the life that would be best for young people in the country (and in the city too), is not to be had in the 1970's. And isn't it a shame?

Delicate Collision

COMMUNES MAY HAVE BEEN last year's "with it" topic, but their time as novelty and sensation has passed. With that decline in public fervor, there seems to have arrived an age of easier and more amicable relations between the established residents of the small New England towns and the young people who choose to dwell in groups among them.

The communards take over the fallow farm once tilled by some old fellow known to everybody in the neighborhood. As long as there has been a town, everybody has known just about what went on on that farm —how well the stock was kept, whose son went for a missionary in Africa, how the spring holds up in droughts.

There's no reason to suppose the good people of the town will cease their wondering just at the moment a dozen strangely accented and oddly dressed, long-haired, unkempt and unmarried kids move into the old Biddle place, or the Thomas brothers' lower farm, or wherever. Truism: everybody always gets talked about in a country village. One need never wonder whether one is a topic of conversation among those waiting around at the laundromat, sitting over a beer at the Frog Pond, leaning on a stack of boxes down at the mill during break. Everybody is. The little old lady who watches TV all day and walks to the post office every evening gets talked about: "She don't do nawthin' but watch TV and walk to the post office." The most prosperous farmer in town gets talked about: "Busy one, he's selling milk!" The gentle and trusting local grocer gets talked about: "God, with the hours he puts in he'd be making a bundle." That sort of gossip, of course, fills the hours and lets everybody know they are living in the same town.

Some topics are more interesting, and given the proper company, they are psychic Lorelei, drawing strong men to yield to temptations-in-mind if not in deed. That, naturally, means Helen, Timmy Grabowski's widow, who fell for some brash young cad only a month after the funeral of her husband, and, trapped by her own values because she sees herself as the rest of the town sees her, has been frenetically leaping from back seat to back seat ever since.

Out here there is still, even among most of the younger men, a sense of decency. It is not really safe to be too coarse when talking about Helen. One just may be judged by one's fantasies, the more so because the gap between talk and action is threateningly short. Put up or shut up, and as most of the men are bearably married, conversations about Helen go just so far.

Not so with discussions about the communards, especially when they first hit town. It's the stuff of every man's secret dreams. In flesh, in his own town, are all them girls, living right out in the open with fellows, going about with long hair, no bras, looking wanton and willing for all the world to see. What of the commune's men?

Clearly, their presence shows that the girls are no prudes. But those guys are barely more than kids. They look weak; they have that damned dirty long hair. "Some night," one of the local bloods might be saying down at the Frog Pond (never saying which night he has in mind), "some night I ought to head up there and have me a talk with some of them girls, take one out for a walk, have a case of beer."

"You'd drink the beer, forget all about the girl, and she'd probably end up shrugging her shoulders and walking home alone," says someone else, poking fun but sustaining the myth that *the girls are willing.*

Cayenne says a fellow from the other side of her town in southern Vermont once gave her a ride in his pickup when she was hitching, drove in silence for ten minutes, then blurted out, "Wanna meet me later tonight, I'll bring some booze?"

Cayenne smiled and said, "Thanks. Thanks but no. I'm too tired. Thanks though," and left the fellow blushing.

So the talk goes on, the more actual contact with the new group, the less speculative the chatter. The real case offers far less to brood about than the fantasy. "They bake all their own bread—six loaves a day, at least!" may be strange to the town's usual habits nowadays, but it bears less thinking about than, "They don't wear no bras."

Within a year, the talk about the new group seems to die down; within two or three, certain strong bonds between the group and individuals in the town develop. Michael, of Magic Farm, works in Harry Sexton's dairy and seems lately to be eating more meals with Harry's family than he does at home. Harry told Michael that he gets asked about the group frequently, because everyone knows he's friends with them. It's been over a year since the drunken joy riders have ceased buzzing Magic Farm at midnight, on Saturdays, yelling and heaving empties out the car windows.

But how awkwardly the acquaintance begins. Each side first lets blossom an entire and wrong-headed vision of its neighbors. The men of the town think what suits them best, the women and old folks brood in general terms about laziness, immorality, rich kids, welfare cheating, the bad influence on the young of the area.

The communards usually are middle class and quite in the habit of moving to new places and making new friends. They mistake curiosity for friendliness, and are always too forward in their first encounters with the local tradesmen and officials. They fantasize pungent country characters, possessed of a "live and let live" attitude that hasn't been seen much around here since the Indians.

A new commune dropped from the sky a few towns west of Clabberville. Recently, in search of new parts for my tractor, I found myself walking in that town for the first time. It's not so different from Clabberville, perhaps a bit smaller, perhaps with land a bit flatter and more fertile.

I walked past the tiny public library, which I'm sure, like the Clabberville library, is filled each afternoon with fat girls and a few shy boys, poring through the *Britan-*

nica Junior and tracing maps of Nebraska and Idaho from the atlas. But there were no kids in the library. They all sat out on the steps, one or two smoking, all of them chattering back and forth, giggling, having quite an animated visit.

They did not cease their chatter as I excused myself and walked up the steps. "One white sock and one blue sock . . ." I heard the most strident of the dumpy girls pronounce. Within was one lone hippie. He was reading the new *Mechanix Illustrated*, sitting gangly and rangy on one of the hard oak chairs. Sure enough, he wore sandals, one white sock and one blue sock. The shock of his presence had forced the kids out on the steps.

The boy smiled affably and confidently at me, then turned back to his magazine. I'm sure he imagined that the high-schoolers always hang out on the front steps of the library, although more likely, he hasn't given them much thought at all. That's all fine. Another few sightings and the kids will be back at work, hippie or no hippie. New Englanders would prove inhospitable to commies or corrupters of their youth, but they have a long tradition of tolerating eccentrics and folks who do things their own way.

The Wendell farm, where a dozen friends of mine farm ten acres of organic vegetables and sell four or five thousand bales of hay each summer, has worked out a nice, wholesome integration with the town. One local luminary brings his bottle there some Saturdays, and ties one on sitting in their kitchen and singing country songs. The local chicken farmer shares tools with them and dumps truckloads of real fine manure there without charge. His kids play at the commune, and some of the teen-agers in town use Wendell's shop and welding equipment to work on their cars.

The old balance has been restored. The farm is worked, not by the Thomas brothers, but by a dozen other folks everyone has seen around for years. They are making a bit of money farming, and everyone knows you have to have a pretty good idea what you are doing to keep farming. The town knows what's going on there, and the farm folk know who they like in town. They have made sufficient peace with the community and may grow old and die there, just like anyone else.

Pig's End

I WALK INTO Jimmy Barlow's garage and one of the wise old men in attendance asks, "What've you been up to?" I say I've been sawing cordwood all day.

"Had an uncle once, but I never knew him, 'cause he died when he was only thirteen —cordwood saw's a dangerous thing," Doc cautions me. Everybody has a horror story about every job you can possibly do on the farm. I suppose it's the rural equivalent of getting-stuck-in-the-elevator stories back in the Big Apple.

Loading corn into the silo? Some helpful neighbor is sure to tell about a fellow who lost his foot when he slipped down the upended dump-truck body ("Like glass, y'know!") and got his foot tangled with the giant auger that shoves chopped corn into the blower. Baling hay? Who will recite the doleful tale of the unnoticed baby crawling in the windrow?

"Jimmy," I say after a while, "I need a few deer slugs for my four-ten shotgun."

"You ain't jacking deer, are you, Mark?" says wise Emil. "I should think there was enough on your hill so as you could wait and get one in season."

"No, not jacking deer," I say. "It's time to butcher the pigs."

"Getting the hair off them's the worst part. You gonna scald them? We had a big scalding tank, a chute leading right up to it. You gotta get the skin scalded enough to loosen the hair, but not so much it sets or turns the skin red," Emil says.

I say I'm planning to skin them first, rather than removing the hair. They've never heard of this and murmur some about it, but it's the common way hog dressing is done on the circle of young people's farms around here. Emil grunts, wants to get back to the question of scalding.

"You know I told you about that chute leading down to the scalding tank? Well, way before I was born, my mother lost her oldest son. He'd been sent out of the barn during the sticking, but he wanted to see what was happening . . ."

I'll spare you the middle of the story. The end tells enough: "Three days. Three days he hung on, down in the hospital, and in the end they say he seemed to stop hurting for long enough to thank the doctor and kiss his mother good-bye . . ."

I'd just finished Ed Sanders' book about the Manson clan. Strange it is to have one of your own kind wandering through that California vale of weirdness, reporting on just what you're wondering about, and then some, and when you're quite satiated with gory information, telling you still more. I'd finished the book in one long sitting three days before the impending butchery.

Then a friend started reading it. One a.m., the first hour of the day of the slaughter, she is still sitting up reading. She's Norwegian and doesn't know all Charlie's macabre slang. "What does it mean, 'snuff out somebody'?" she asks. I'm half asleep and don't answer. I've spent the evening reading the "Swine" chapter in each of four or five farm chronicles. Bromfield likes pigs. Tetlow likes to butcher them, is proud of his economy. The *Encyclopaedia Britannica* says, "The origin of the pig is shrouded in mystery." They say, "A mature pig has forty-four teeth, carries its head low, and eats, drinks, and breathes close to the ground." One of the books—I can't recall which in my drowsy jumble of thoughts—says the domestic pig is closely related to swamp-dwelling wild boars of Africa. I fall asleep.

I dream that I am creeping through an African swamp, close to the ground, and that hunters in boats are trying to snuff me out. I wake up and I am afraid. Stevie says when you die, God eats you, and it's the same for pigs. I have never killed anything before. Last year Walter the dog killed the pigs for me. This year they have fattened well.

Pig One is a friend of mine who comes to the fence to have her ears scratched. Pig Two is shy and has always kept her distance. One is a bully, rooting wherever Two starts to root. If I throw them rotten apples in the pen, they fight over one apple, then they fight over a second apple, and so on until One has eaten seven apples and Two has eaten three apples; it's the reason for keeping two pigs. My pigs were born in May. In the first week of November, One weighs two hundred and fifty pounds and Two

59

weighs two hundred, and they are ready for the freezer, the curing crock, the smokehouse.

Pigs are all of a single mind. They want to eat. They want there to be lotsa good eats. They want to be warm and to have enough room so they can sleep in one place and excrete in some far corner after they eat. One and Two have lived inside a rectangular fence built on skids. Hourly, they eat, sleep, excrete, and eat again. When no food is at hand, they furrow deep gouges in the ground with their noses.

Whenever they had rooted the ground into mud, I'd hitch the tractor to the pen and tow it to a clean patch of turf. They would then squeal like a jazz saxophone on high runs and chase each other in circles, from the sheer joy of having a new green swath to snuffle through. Five times in their brief lives I moved their pen. First it would be six weeks before I'd have to move it, then four, and then in only two weeks they had excavated trenches and gullies and taken to flipping snoutsful of mud over their grain trough. The pen was last moved a week before their martyrdom. The six tilled bare patches they leave fertile and free of weeds will grow corn to feed next summer's pigs. They are their own legacy and have given this small work besides.

I have not killed any animal before—I now recall—save for one porcupine who got into the food sack once while we were camping. I threw a work boot at him and broke his neck, quite by accident.

Last year my mother urged me to take from her her seventeen-year-old dog, weak and failing by the day from cancer. She said it would die happily "in the country," knowing full well that a dog wants most to be with its mistress. It came and immediately languished, lying under a maple in the June sun, so sick it could not move to shake the vulturelike flies from itself. Late in the afternoon, it was swaddled in them, as if wearing blue armor, the buzzing sound a continuous, hollow harmonic hymn. I couldn't take it and called Rex, asking him if he'd come up the hill with his pistol. I dug her grave, he came, and at the last moment, I panicked, handed him back his gun, and fled behind the barn. I awaited the thunder of artillery (not to mention the stern voice of Judgment), heard instead one short *thwit*, the sound a tough city kid makes spitting stylishly into the gutter with tongue rolled. I thought, "It's confusing enough to decide the time of some creature's death, but having once decided, surely it's not proper to ask someone else to carry out that decision for me."

Thus did I approach the time of hog butchering with some inner chaos. Yet I somehow do not feel spiritually eligible for vegetarianism. It would be an act so much kinder and more God-fearing than the other acts of my callow existence that it has seemed absurd whenever I've tried it.

However, I share with many other city expatriates the conviction that if you are going to eat meat, and if you have the facilities to raise and kill it yourself, that's what you should be willing to do. If I buy meat from the market, not only is it adulterated with the hormones and medications commonly employed in commercial meat production, but it is nevertheless flesh killed on my behalf by someone else. My decision to kill the pigs myself was a way of acknowledging just what I am doing when I am eating what was once quick.

I asked my friends to come—John, whose calm and decent nature lends equilibrium in tight times; Terry, who is a matter-of-fact butcher, self-taught from government pamphlets, and proud of his competence; Verandah, to offer a note of dignity; Cindy, Andy, and Richard, to come up with a few coarse yucks at the right time; and Doug, to tell us all how it looks from over there.

Doug came dressed in impeccable whites and remained unsullied throughout the carnage. Terry was in a rush. I went down to the pen accompanied and, working too fast for second thoughts, loaded the gun, cocked the hammer, held the barrel half a foot from the head of Two, and pulled the trigger. The sound and the shock of the gun against the shoulder were one. The small hole centered an inch above the eyes of Two, two or three bristly hairs leaning into it, seemed a circumstance removed from the shot, some facial feature that had always been there. Two knelt instantly, not tipping to one side or the other. Then her hind legs gave way. She rolled on her side, the legs flicking a full minute in the air, as if she was trying to walk away. Terry entered the pen and cut the neck veins to help keep the meat free from clotted blood. What spilled on the ground was drunk by Pig One, who stayed calm and curious throughout the death of her sister.

As for me, I trembled for some minutes while Andy gazed at me. One of the first coherent thoughts to enter my mind after the sound of the shot annoyed me terribly: "I will write about this trembling tomorrow and will feel ostentatious when I do it." I became calm as Two ceased to move. We loaded her on a sled and dragged it with the tractor through the snow from pen to barn. Terry splayed her hind legs apart with a stick notched at either end and lashed through leg incisions to each gambrel tendon.

Then we hoisted the pig, head down, from the beam with block and tackle, gutted, skinned, and decapitated it, saving such entrails as we felt we could deal with (nearly everything is usable if one has the stamina, but we forsook the intestines and stomach, and took the other organs for sausage). I sawed the carcass in two, right down the center of the backbone, and the halves, weighing seventy-five pounds each, were taken into the house for butchering. Then we went back and did the same with Number One.

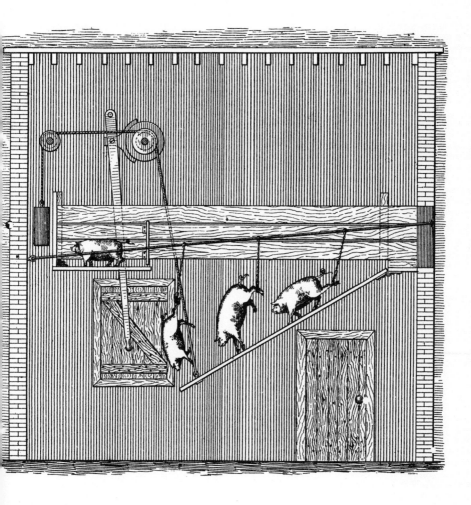

I felt just as bad and left the scene before the pig was stuck, walking out into the field with my back to the pen, thinking the same damn thought a second time, and feeling that my life is converted into something other than the sum of my experiences because I am delivering up relics of it as I write. I went down and drove the tractor to the barn a second time and later helped carry half of Pig One to the kitchen.

It was somewhat easier from there. Once a pig was reduced to sides of meat, everyone felt calmer. We cut Pig Two into roasts, chops, sides of bacon, hams, and sausages, and then stopped to eat, enervated and glutted from the experience. We feasted on pork chops and broiled pig livers.

As we finished supper the cavalry came, being my friends Allen, weaver, carpenter, farmer, master of all trades, and Dotty, enduring, direct, also an ace weaver, a good carpenter, and otherwise purveyor of efficient bustle. They came in on this grotesque crowd, spattered with gore, gaunt with hours of hard work and hard thoughts, gnawing on the bones of their first victim.

They took the situation in hand and soon had the uncut sides of Pig One hung to cool in the attic, the cut meats spread to cool on a table next to them. Then we drank and sang and slept and the next morning the world seemed far kinder than it had for days.

Allen knew how to do everything well, which relieved me of the gnawing thought that having done this deed, I was nevertheless too much of an amateur to make good use of what I had brought to earth. Under his direction, we rubbed the hams and bacons in salt, ginger, thyme, and brown sugar, packed them in a great crock, and left them to cure.

We quickly finished butchering Pig One, wrapped the

meat of both pigs for freezing, mixed several gallons of sausage, buried what we couldn't use, and ate spareribs for supper.

Once it was over, it seemed less of an event, of course. Unless I know better by then, I'll probably raise more pork. I'll probably regret the slaughter and I will probably recover enough to enjoy the meat as I have this year.

Chicken Shit People

ALTHOUGH FOOD PRODUCTION capability in the USA has been climbing steadily as the population increases and lucrative export markets swell, the percentage of the population involved in agriculture has been dropping for many years. About the turn of the century about seventy percent of all Americans were farming. Now I think the figure is nearer seven percent. This fact naturally reflects a considerable alteration in the social structure and the quality of life of the nation, and has been determined largely by economic factors.

It's basically cheaper for big farmers to produce food, and they can make things quite uncomfortable for small farmers. At the same time, other labor markets compete for workers once destined for lives in the fields, and before many years have passed, most of the farmers in a town have their sons working in the factories and their land sold to the few hardy and enterprising operators still growing food. The biggest operators farm the best land, let the rest go back to woods (Massachusetts woodland acreage has more than doubled in the past seventy-five years).

The task of producing food will occupy still fewer hands in the future. One consequence of this concentration is a standardization of available produce, and of the sometimes unhealthy but expedient practices used in growing it. Modern agribusiness can deliver thousands of tons of blemish-free canteloupes (the leading type is in fact called "Supermarket"), but they will all be of varieties chosen for long shelf-life and resistance to rot and denting in crates, not for their nutritional value or good taste. They will be grown with the use of herbicides and chemical fertilizers, not to make better melons, but to make melons more cheaply.

It's not hard to find the effects of the standardization and concentration of food growing right here in Clabberville. There's a roadside stand set up by an old farmer named Bishop Steward which offers plum tomatoes, four or five breeds of regular tomatoes, and yellow pear-shaped tomatoes as well. Last year, for the first time, Bishop had to take part of his harvest down to the wholesale vegetable market near Springfield and sell it in competition with the regular growers. He got no premium for variety—in fact he couldn't move the yellow ones—no premium for his craft, and he barely broke even on his summer's tomato harvest. The following summer he put in half his usual crop, just what he could move at the stand to old customers and no more, and who's to blame him?

All this explanation is just to set the stage for the extraordinary enterprise of the chicken shit people. The chicken shit people are five men and one woman who have started up a three-hundred-acre organic farm in central New York State. The magnitude of that ambition is astounding.

Jim and George and Ira have all farmed before. They were part of the largest commercial organic farm I know about around here—raising about a dozen acres of corn, melons, potatoes, and a few other vegetables on a cooperative basis. They made enough to live on, working long hours and depending on their numbers (about ten) to make up for their shortage of specialized machinery, a practice not open to straight farmers because of high labor costs. That farm is still going on, but Jim and George and Ira have all left for the big time.

"I've traveled all over," said George, "lived in a lot of different scenes (he once taught English in Saudi Arabia) and whatever I do, I keep coming back to farming because it makes me happy." Ira is a beefy, whip-smart Jewish kid who still has some incompletes at Amherst, and who has in the past few years taught himself to build houses and rebuild old truck engines because Amherst wouldn't teach him those things.

And Jim, at twenty-three, has earned the respectful nickname of "Doc"—he says, "It won't stick, but it's nice"—because when machines break he keeps smiling and soon has them back in operation. He is a master welder with a flair for improvised repairs that keep working, and the energy to keep hard at a job as long as there's light to see. George has brought in his friends Caesar and Dick, both young students in agriculture school. Caesar's mother kept an organic garden for years ("She never called it that, but it was") and this gave him the hint that the ag school fertilizer-pesticide-herbicide method might not be the only True Way.

Jim bought an old gravel dump truck for $750—the

kind you see on heavy road-building projects—which had been retired from road-building and then retired from a long subsequent career with a local contracter. He "got it running good again"—a phrase that smooths over weeks of anguish and dirty work—and set out for the new farm with Linda, who had put an ad in *Organic Gardening* asking for a summer job on a farm. She got more than she bargained for, and is now a member in good standing of the new enterprise.

Central New York State is real big-time farm country. Having just come back from there, I wonder all the more at the stubborn New Englanders who continue to work their three acres of corn on the side of some hill, and seven acres of good hay won from the little shoulder of bottomland above the river. These New York farms have single fields of forty and fifty acres of beautiful rolling land, and on the dairy farms, herds of several hundred milkers are not uncommon.

After months of searching, the five men had located an abandoned place high up a dirt road, with poor barns falling in, a poor house, salvageable, but it's cold in the winter, and two hundred acres of lovely tillable open land rolling across three hills, nearly one hundred acres of pasture, and about fifty acres of woodlot. They got it for about a third the asking price of a working farm.

Next they found an old chicken farm nearby, and for the price of a beer down at the Brown Beaver, the old man who used to work it let them have a veritable treasure in chicken shit. So George's old Farmall H, and an old M that came with the farm, and Jim's wonderful 1935 John Deere A, a two-cylinder job with external flywheel and hand clutch, trundled in a brigade down to the chicken farm, followed by the resurrected dump truck. They scraped and loaded ton after ton of chicken shit, rumbled home again and again through the crossroads of bar, gas station, post office, and general store, called the center of town, and won their name, "the Chicken Shit People."

At first the local bloods griped about the disservice those longhairs (not Jim—he's the resident townie) were perpetrating, bringing that nasty ammonia smell into town, and talked about dumping a load on the front steps of the farmhouse some night. Soon they were drinking and playing pool with our heroes, and not long after that were coming up and lending a hand haying or helping to put together a "new" wagon. Willet Produce is the first new scene in town since tractors came into style, and it has not been long in gaining a welcome.

The local equipment dealer came up and offered them the opportunity to try out a mammoth tractor with wheels higher than a man stands, which pulls four plows at once through the toughest sod. It got a sore test right away. Dick seized the opportunity to turn over thirty acres of old acid sod, dense with orchard grass, strawberries, blackberries, and buttercups in the low spots—a field nearly a mile and a half in perimeter.

Five of us went out, paced off a centerline at different points across the field and stood in the tall grass marking each spot as the tractor lugged down the line. At dusk

70

the tractor finally roared up to the house. Dick grabbed some supper while Caesar and Clem from town raided the junk-car lot in back of the barn, came back with two sealed-beam headlamps, and roped and wired them into place. Then it was back to the field. At dawn I was awakened by the sound of their return from work. Two others took their place, and by noon the next day, the field was done, ready for harrowing and the sowing of buckwheat. Then Linda drove the tractor back down to the equipment dealer and thanked him for the "free home trial."

The seed was combined late in September. It commanded a premium price and helped pay for a new tractor they can use at a slower pace.

The buckwheat also served as an effective "smother" crop. It is a prolific spreader and does well in spent soil. It's a frost-sensitive annual, and if the seed is collected, one is left a clear field of stubble in spring, suitable for planting to corn or good mowing.

They also sowed winter wheat and put in several acres of melons and feed corn, some other vegetables, have taken twenty acres of hay, and set out a king-sized house garden. It seems a miracle, but the new farm is underway—one of the first eastern efforts to supply the demand for new health foods, grown as small private growers used to grow them before the age of standard quality. Their life-style and handiness have allowed them to do it on nearly no money, save what they borrowed from friends and fathers as down payment on the farm.

But it is rare. Few farmers understand the peculiar marketing practices necessary to make a go selling to consumers of organic food. And few freaks understand the ways of farming well enough to do the job. Of those who do, fewer still want to work that hard. I think it will be a long time before enterprises like Willet Produce are common enough to lower the premium prices of natural foods, prices now determined by the need to import grain from Texas, meat from Arkansas, and vegetables from California.

The Evil-oution
of Clabberville

CLABBERVILLE HAS BEEN most kindly left out of most of the great social movements of the past twenty years. Vaguely Republican and generally anticommunist by dint of early training and long habit, the citizens have had cause neither to question their convictions nor to take themselves very seriously as political beings.

They are most directly affected by local politics—by the election of the town selectmen, fence viewers, and the boards of assessors and education. And these nonpartisan jobs, more nuisance than glory, have nearly always gone to competent gentlemen from families known to most everyone in town.

Several fortuitous circumstances have, until recently, saved Clabbervillians from the baleful temptations of avarice and greed. Perhaps the main good fortune is geographical accident. Located in the rough hills half an hour by car from the county seat, Clabberville only re-

73

cently was included in the expanding net of improved roads which make more and more of the state available to the desecrations of outside money.

The local mill, which now manufactures felted paper products such as antimacassars for the backs of railway seats, outer wrappers for sanitary napkins, and disposable sheets for army field hospitals, has for the past fifty years proved a convenient sop for any labor not taken up by farming. As rising costs and stable wholesale market prices have driven all but a dozen dairy farmers out of business, the mill has taken advantage of the reliable and skilled supply of workers.

So far, the mill has not passed out of family hands. But the surplus of jobs no longer exists—workers laid off at other plants within commuting distance have filled the open positions. Nothing is so certain as it used to be; a few families, who wouldn't have dreamed of such a thing a few years back, are even on welfare.

The Farmer's Everyday Book, published not far from Clabberville in 1851, cautions that "If a boy sleeps an hour too much each day, he will lose fourteen or fifteen days in a year . . . let him calculate how much he might earn in the time now wasted in sleep." Such is the heritage of industriousness under which even the poorest families of the area labor.

It has long been thought shameful to accept the largesse of the state while still able-bodied—an application of ideals perhaps appropriate during the age of subsistence farming, but inappropriate and frequently humiliating in these times of nationally managed economy, when employment is more related to the progress of our international tyranny than it is to a man's good character.

"One of the most degrading and offensive modes of providing for the poor," says the *Everyday Book*, "is the annual exposure of them at auction; not indeed quite like the public sale of cattle and swine, to see who will give the most for them, but to see who will maintain these poor creatures at the lowest rates: that is, in effect, to see who has the art of keeping life in them at the least possible cost."

The practice, of course, has long since been stopped. But the feeling of shame in taking public doles still persists. Being out of work is no easier in Clabberville than it is in the inner city.

Coming at this time when prices are going up so much faster than local wages, the economic bait held out by tourists and "summer people" is particularly tempting. The bait has considerably upset the old social order in ways that the outsiders would find quite surprising, if they cared to examine them.

Up until recently, the town has been pretty much all of a class. There have always been a few exceptions of course—the mill executives, occasional entrepreneurs, and artists drawn by the region's remoteness.

When land was of little real value and was within reach of any young man who wanted to farm, there was little to separate the workers in the mill from their uncles and brothers on the farms. The history of the generations of Clabberville is full of stories of men who worked in the mill for ten years, carried the mail for another ten, and farmed from then on until they retired to live with their children.

Now things are different. Farmers are suddenly rich men, in an odd manner of speaking, and isolated from the rest of the town by the changing nature of their craft. Where ten neighbors might once have helped each other with haying, mechanization has now wiped out the smallest farmers and left those still in business pretty much to themselves. A farmer and his son working hard can take in up to five hundred bales a day. The neighbors work in factories and couldn't help even if they were needed.

But most important, the farmer's acreage has suddenly a greatly increased value—it is in demand as country retreat, as building site, and as timberland. I would guess that the average farmer in 1925 might have had $3,000 or $4,000 invested in farm, stock, and tools on the premises. Now I can't think of a farmer in town who couldn't auction his stock and machinery for nearly $20,000 and get another $50,000 for house and land—and that's the poorest farmer.

So as his cousin in the factory finds himself suddenly unsure about the future of his job, the farmer finds himself tempted to sell out and place himself and his children on the same labor market. But good jobs are scarce, and none are sure.

Once everybody who grew up here expected to stay. Now many young people expect to leave. Even the ex-farmers are on the move. One I knew has sold out and used his fortune to move to Maine and invest in a still profitable farming venture there. Another has gone to work managing a farm in Ohio, while his son has moved to Boston, where he works as a telephone repairman. And of those who stay, more and more turn to jobs which make them dependent on the money brought in from elsewhere by skiers and lovers of mountain air.

New antique shops and flea markets abound, carpenters and house painters devote most of their time to patchwork for out-of-town owners, where there was once no call for these services at all because people did such jobs themselves.

Lest I exaggerate the progress of the fragmentation— the trend has yet to make Clabberville an inhospitable place to live. A sort of uncharitable intimacy still pervades local dealings. Everyone knows everyone, and most often, some blood tie can be found linking anyone with anyone else. The thief has been known as a thief for thirty years. The fellow who kicks his cows and starves his horses can't keep it a secret, nor can the lady with money in her mattress.

It may be that when confronted with outsiders, this sharing of secrets will draw the "locals" (as they are destined to be known) closer together. But I don't see how life in Clabberville can continue as decently as it has up until now.

Making the Good Move

To MOVE TO the country and grow a nice garden is one thing, to move to the country and farm, quite another, and few people not raised to that sort of life are actually interested in doing it. With the exception of my friends the "Chicken Shit People" who have started the large organic farm in New York State, I don't know anyone who has even attempted it.

A real estate agent here once said to me that selling country property to young people was a matter of interpreting dreams. She said that the hardest thing to do is to sort through the façade of practical bluster and get to the vision of what life ought to be like at some ideal property. If she has such a property listed, it might be "double the price limit of the interested party," as she put it, "but they will buy it anyway."

You have no idea how many times each week, early spring to late fall, local brokers hear some hearty shaggy fellow asking after "a rundown farmhouse—nothing fancy, you know—I'm pretty handy. I want some land to be with it."

There are no rundown farmhouses left in this region and save for a rare few, there haven't been since 1967 or so. It pays to fix them up and if the rundown farmer doesn't know that, a neighbor or broker who does will buy the house from him and do the job. Nowadays $30,000 is the lowest possible country farm price hereabouts and that's rare.

A SWINDLER SECURING THE SIGNATURE OF HIS VICTIM.

Dealers get six to ten percent of the selling price— from the seller, but it's always added to the asking price—so it's cheaper to buy directly, perhaps by advertising in the local papers. It's not likely you'll find anything without a dealer. Most sellers go through one to avoid the mysteries of the sale. But perhaps your friends who already live in the country have heard of someone who is selling privately. They won't necessarily tell you because they have already been asked by a hundred people they barely know for the same thing.

If you want the best deal, do try to forage for yourself. You may hear about the place you want from just anyone, but most likely it will be from local people with whom you have formed some sort of special relationship —people who have decided they want you in town. Perhaps the local schoolteacher wants her three-year-old to join the nursery school you plan to start, or perhaps the local horse trader has you marked as a potential cus-

79

tomer, if you can find a house for yourself and a barn to keep the nag in.

Most of the people who buy farms around here nowadays are from the city. Local folk can't afford them. There are two economies in operation really. One you will hear about through brokers, and another comes into play when, say, a farmer sells out to his son-in-law or the garage man agrees to order a new battery for you at cost because he's been fixing your pickup for ten years now and it still runs good. But it's getting so the sums are too large for a friendly family house-selling business.

Some city buyers pose a grave danger to the souls of country tradesmen—graver than sex and graver than alcohol. Blindly, they turn competent workers into servants. Services around here still are far superior to their city counterparts. But they are fading fast. Ray the butcher hand-slices his bacon, for eighty-nine cents a pound and only charges you seventy-five cents if he's cutting the end of a slab. His hamburger is mostly meat. A plumber sent his apprentice out for free to help me stop a leaky toilet because he figured in a few years I'll buy an oil burner from him, which by the way I won't and I told him so. Wonderful Mrs. Kenmore in the stationery store puts aside a copy of *Fur, Fish and Game* (fantastic inside savvy on the ways of beasts—the trade journal of professional trappers) in case (not because) I want it, and when we were making vinegar, she brought me some mother from the top of her jug. The garage man will mend a tractor tire in half an hour for a buck. The town snowplow will come at six a.m. if you have to get to work. Even a thoroughly objectionable electrician who was here briefly last winter and who said he likes to shoot dogs, put in, for free and without asking, a new switch to the cellar light because he noticed the old one was breaking.

Of course it won't be many years now before there's no time and no need, no joy in this kind of service. Up until now, everyone here was about the same kind of poor. Everyone knows each other and knew each other's grandfathers. And engines, electricity, and plumbing are everybody's business and no mystery to anyone. So what tradesman is going to fast-talk his neighbor, whose sister is married to his second cousin, and who knows pretty well how to do the repair himself? It wouldn't even occur to such a man to be other than honest.

Now, because more and more local income is earned from city folks buying and fixing "second" homes, things are rapidly changing. The effects of this influx were anticipated by Helen and Scott Nearing and very very amply discussed in their book, *Living the Good Life*. Typical of the early fifties, they saw the social problem as a "how to" question (the book is subtitled, "How to Live Sanely and Simply in a Troubled World"), and remained quite optimistic that neighborly good character could lead to reorganization of the social structure and restore such mutual aid as once existed among rural people. I wonder if the Nearings still maintain their optimism today. They were forced out of their beloved back-hills valley in southern Vermont (their farm faced Stratton Mountain) by ski development and thwarted in their attempts to involve their neighbors with each other in mutually advantageous community projects. In fact, the Nearings anticipated their own demise in their analysis of the efforts of city folks on rural life, which I quote at length—it is so eloquently to the point.

We started as "summer folk" who are usually looked on by the native population as socially untouchable and a menace to agriculture . . . In so far as summer residents occupy productive land, take it out of use and let it revert to brush, they are a detriment to the agriculture of the state . . . Another thing the summer residents do to Vermont agriculture is put a premium on factory goods and specialties shipped in from out of state, have them carried in the stores and thus help to persuade Vermont residents that it is easier and cheaper to get dollars, exchange them for canned goods sold in the stores, and abandon long-established gardens in the course of the turn-over. Thus the state is made less dependent on its own agriculture, and more dependent on dollars, many of which will be used to buy out-of-state produce.

If this process goes far enough, Vermont will develop a suburban or vacationland economy, built on the dollars of those who make their income elsewhere and spend part of it during a few weeks or months of the Vermont summer. Such economy is predominantly parasitic in terms of production, although income and expense accounts may be in balance. Carried to its logical conclusion, it would make Vermonters sell their labor-power to summer residents, mowing their lawns and doing their laundry, thus greatly reducing their own economic self-dependence. Such an economy may attract more cheap dollars to the state, but it will hardly produce self-reliant men.

Nevertheless I think, after carefully searching my heart and conjuring the least unpleasant direction rural society might take, that it is fine when some city folks make the move to the country—providing they avoid making things worse than they already are. Let them not be like one mogul old couple we'll call the Manacottis.

One town east of here the Manacottis bought an old mill—barely more than a broken-down barn by the time they "made their find." They put no less than $40,000 into it and succeeded in getting it to look like a new suburban imitation colonial. Their acre of summer fun squats right between the houses of the former mill owner and his cousin, both of whom have been there for thirty or thirty-five years. Even while they were building, the valley was full of talk that they didn't know what they were doing—for the same price they could have gotten a whole farm, or at least some privacy, and they wanted a water pump twice as large as they needed, and they drilled a well when spring water was right at hand. The first thing they did when they moved in was to hire a local farmer, a fellow modest, well liked, helpful, private, and businesslike, to seed their lawn and plant them a garden. He did just that, and next time he saw Manacotti, he said he was done.

"What do I owe you for that work?" says Manacotti.

"Twenty dollars ought to pay me for my time and tractor," says the forthright farmer.

"You did a good job, my good man, so I'm giving you thirty-five."

Says the forthright farmer to me the next day: "How the hell did he know whether I did a good job?"

The devil in golf clothes may pass summers in Manacotti's mill, but down the road about three sees ("What's a see?" the city fellow asks the old farmer. "Well, you go down the road about as far as you can see . . .") reside some newly winged angels, by the names of Phillip and Micky Laamb, and children.

The tale of their move is about as happy as one can be in these restless times. It starts off with big Hans Kruger marrying a farmer's daughter, and joining in the operation of her father's farm. Kruger soon bought the next house down the road. Things worked out well; the farm became one of the best in the area, milking one hundred and twenty Holsteins under the direction of Kruger's father-in-law, a fellow of absolute brilliance whose dry wit makes his presence a series of entertaining surprises. The trouble with Kruger was not in-laws but bursitis, and he recently had to leave the farming operation because he couldn't continue to milk. Enter the Laambs, looking for property. Exit the Krügers, headed for Florida.

Phil wants to grow a big garden to feed the family, and he wants to milk goats. Said Mrs. Kruger, "He says he wants to farm, but I don't think he knows too much about it."

The misunderstanding was partially semantic. The Laambs don't want to farm, they want to garden, by local usage, and keep an animal. This practice is still so common among factory workers from farm families that it is not thought of as farming at all—just living.

Yet it is the new adventure of the Laambs' life, and will likely occupy their full attention at least through their first year. They will soon transcend whatever urban fantasy has led them here, tempering their breaths of good sweet air with ragweed sneezes. They will undergo trials of goats that eat workshirts, and tractors that won't start to plow the snow just when the baby has to be taken to the doctor and it's ten below zero out. But the garden will come up, and sooner or later the goats will give good milk, the income-producing home crafts will be underway, and they will be able to appraise their new life. I figure they will like it, because they are both really interested in doing what they plan to do, have the independence and discipline to do it to their own satisfaction, and most important, they will undoubtedly become full members of the community, with kids in school, friends to visit, and, of course, much they want to learn from their neighbors. No Manacottis, they!

Still, the Laambs' future here is not all rosy. They have these changing times to cope with. The ugliest town meeting in two hundred years of local history took place here not long ago. Frightened by the tremendous load imposed on town facilities just across the state line by Vermont burn-scheme developments, Clabberville passed two-acre zoning a few months ago. Then local land, lumber, and real estate interests realized what loss would someday be theirs if they couldn't sell quarter-acre plots with imitation chalets stuck on them. So they made up a lot of sanctimonious reasons about freedom for the town to decide its own future in view of future trends, and they organized a revote on the zoning question. They seemed about to pack the meeting with uncles and to railroad through an open season for land speculation. But a hastily assembled coalition of conservation-minded local folks and a few hermits recently transplanted from elsewhere just managed to stand them off. It's only the opening skirmish and the other team is bound to win sooner or later. When that happens, I—along with the Laambs and the few other resident new-age recluses—may have to abandon Clabberville to those harbingers of a profitable bad scene to come—the Manacottis. Perhaps we'll go farther back where it's colder and less accessible still.

Christopher the anthropologist tells me the same thing happened with Indians. He was saying how a Caraja Indian he knew in Brazil would swat killer mosquitoes in slow motion with a dab of one finger, he knew the beasts' habits so well. I said they have had thousands of years to figure mosquitoes out.

No sir, he said, do you think any tribe is going to be crazy enough to live in a swamp when there's rich coastal land to be had? Before the Portuguese came to Brazil, Indians played where Rio squats today.

Same with New York, of course. Vermont and the Berkshire regions may be lovely to the eye, but can you imagine how nice Prospect Park would be with, say, three farms and ninety-six Holsteins occupying the whole of it. It will soon seem remarkable when we tell our grandchildren that we remember when there were farms only ten minutes from downtown Clabberville. My grandmother remembers farms in Brooklyn, so why not?

Country Fairs

BEFORE THE ADVENT of horse-drawn haying equipment—mowers, tedders, rakes, and hay loaders—farming was very much more of a communal affair. The fine *Book of Country Things* describes one neighborly custom practiced in southern Vermont.

The man that got his haying done first always shouldered his scythe and fork, and started down the road to the next man. He would start in there, and when he finished that up he would go on to the next man. There wasn't much of any money in it, it was just a neighborly thing to do. A man would get his board, and his neighbor would help him out with *his* haying.

When people do hard work together, they soon come to know each other's tricks and foibles, generosity and strength. There's no putting on airs after six or seven hours in the hot sun, and the man who can start up a good laugh at a time like that goes a long way toward making everyone happier to be out there. I figure those Dummerston farmers got to liking each other so well they fixed up a few other times to get together, such as the Fourth of July, some kind of harvest time fair, and a winter church supper as well.

When they got together, the usual thing was to have competitions and contests, judged by the elderly notables of the town, to determine who was the strongest fellow, who could shoot the straightest, who could plow the straightest furrow, who could scythe a swath of hay truest and fastest, and, for that matter, who grew the nicest beans or the fattest pumpkin.

Says the *Book of Country Things*:

Gramp won the Dummerston scything championship in a contest to see who could mow a given distance in a certain time with a perfect swath. They had judges to see that the swath was perfectly even. Two men would start on a level, probably ten feet apart, and mow their way up the left side of the field; then at the far end they would turn to the right and mow across the end, then turn to the right again and mow their way back. If the inside man could "mow the other man out of his swath" by getting to the end of the field first, so the outside man couldn't turn to the right without crossing the inside man's swath, then the inside one was a pretty good man. I don't believe anyone ever mowed Grandpa out of his swath.

Now to my way of thinking that's a thrilling contest. I try to imagine the equivalent for some of the city dwellers who might be reading this. Say two accountants copying and toting figures beginning from opposite ends of the same ledger sheet, and the one who gets so far ahead of the other one that he adds up a column of the other one's figures is said to be "clearing the other man's balance." I don't believe anyone ever cleared Grandpa's balance.

The old country fairs do still exist. The best ones are the small local events which are not likely to be publicized because they are not money-making tourist attractions but still meaningful local celebrations. If you are lucky enough to happen upon one, usually late in August or early in September, you are sure to have a good time, say, looking over the blue-ribbon parsnips and wondering why they are so much better than that other bunch that didn't rate with the vegetable judges at all.

The larger fairs are sometimes fun too, though they can be gross midway shyster carnival operations relocated in the hills for a few days. At the Bondville, Vermont, fair, once a large and joyous occasion which had the misfortune to be located in a town turned upside down by the marvelous good fortune of ski development, I saw a sight you will hardly believe. Drunk farmers paid two bucks and slipped into a seedy tent with a trailer stage, where they watched "the girlie show"— one girl who danced a brief and artless strip and then dared the fellows to eat her out (I think the vernacular is applicable here), until a couple of them did just that. Perhaps that is traditional too.

At the larger fairs, the vegetable judging and the crafts exhibitions are likely to have been discontinued years ago. But one event which has hung on throughout the New England fair circuit is horse drawing. This is an event with a long tradition. The beautifully written English chronicle of Suffolk farming, *Ask the Fellows Who Cut the Hay* (by George E. Evans, Faber, London) contains a fine description of an early eighteenth-century horse-drawing match. The newspaper notice for it read:

On Thursday, July 29th, there will be a Drawing at Ixworth Pickarel for a piece of plate 45 shillings value, and they that will bring five horses or mares may put in for it; and they that can draw 20 of the best and fairest pulls with their reins up, and they that can carry the greatest weight over the block with fewest pulls shall have the said plate, by such judges as the masters of the teams shall choose. You are to meet at 12 o'clock and put in your name (or else be debarred from drawing it) and subscribe half-a-crown to be paid to the second best team . . . The trial is made with a wagon loaded with sand, the wheels sunk a little into the ground, with blocks of wood laid before them to increase the difficulty.

A regular group of several dozen New England farmers still keep competitive drawing horses as a hobby. Some will find them useful for work they do as well as or better than tractors—plowing steep hillsides, drawing a vat of maple sap through the snow. But for the most part, the work the horses do, plus the prizes they win at a fair here and there, still does not fully compensate the owners for their costs in keeping the animals and trucking them to the fairs.

Nowadays the contestants draw a skid loaded with sacks of sand for fifteen feet. After a few rounds, the skid (called a stone boat) is so heavily laden that no team can draw it all the way, and then whichever draws it the longest stretch wins.

Most of the audience seems to find horse drawing quite slow to watch for hours, so people come and go as the contest progresses. Only the big final draw of the heaviest class will attract a full complement. The beasts stand harnessed up in their fancy rigging, the whip cracks and the animals rear and back to hook into the load, then nearly drop to their knees in concert as they strain to lug it forward a few steps.

The audience no longer works with horses every day, and because of that, the match isn't the same as it used to be. But it's quite another story with the modern equivalent of the ancient contest—the tractor pull.

First thing that happened to me at the Cincinattus, New York, July the Fourth tractor pull was that I heard a good joke. This farmer he's fixing his mowing machine, see. He's cursing and swearing and throwing his wrenches down because he can't seem to get it working right. And in the middle of all this, a city fellow comes up, watches him for a while, points to the mowing machine, and says, "What's that, farmer, an automobile?" And the farmer he shakes his head and says, "Nope, it's an ought-to-mow-grass, 'cept it won't."

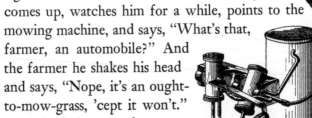

I joined the crowd sizing up the entered vehicles, which, as the judges wrote in the notice of the contest, "may have no other weights or other devices attached than are normally used in everyday fieldwork." Four classes, by weight, are required to draw a stone boat until the tractor wheels slip, the engine stalls, or the front end lifts more than eighteen inches off the ground (a dangling length of light chain affixed to the front axle of a tractor before its draw indicates the front end lift).

It lasted two hours, and the crowd, about two hundred strong, stayed interested from beginning to end. Although one might think it's just a contest between machines, driving skill determined the victories in every class—it's quite a trick to balance off slipping the wheels and stalling the engine by keeping the power on just enough to move the load. The tuning and care of the tractor affect the outcome as well.

The contest was between machines used every day in the field by the farmers who drove them in the contest. It was a meaningful test of skill related to the ordinary lives of the audience, and it was fun. It must have been more fun yet for those who knew the competitors.

A Rich Old Trader

THERE AREN'T MANY rich folk around Clabberville. During the fin de siècle, wilderness divi-
sion, one might have witnessed the tail end of
a tradition of gracious rural moguls, akin to
the patronizing princes of southern planta-
tions. These were the mill owners, whose man-
ufactoriums employed all those for miles around
who had not cast their fortunes with the land.

As the national conglomerates began collecting companies or perhaps even before, who knows anymore, resident mill owners became a rare bunch. Who was left
with money? Precious few, because there was simply
very little to be made from the rocky ground, and the
rapers of roaring rivers and wise workers had skedaddled
to the big cities, reappearing only for summer watering
and occasional auditing of their due. Aside from the doctors, lawyers, mill owners, and certain come-lately ex-
pansionist merchants and loggers, few went hungry and

no one had much. If that sounds like fun, the romantic feeling is inspired only by the passing of enough years to leave hazy the details of daily life.

Through this poverty, there arose an occasional renegade whose ambition and cool temper, ingenuity and cold-bloodedness, tenacity, good fortune, guts, brains, connections, character, and good health were such that he got filthy rich in spite of it all. We'll call ours Smith. He's near ninety now and is not only alive but still active. Everybody in Clabberville knows the old man, and everyone has some story to relate about his eccentric habits, his fortune, his generosity. No one has ever allowed that he cheated them, drove them or their pappy from home when they didn't have the rent, ended up owning their family homestead when they couldn't meet the midwinter installment on the mortgage, although all these may well have happened too.

One upstanding lady whose husband used to hunt with Smith came the closest to uttering aspersion. "Smith?" she said, "I guess it hurts a man sometimes when it comes right down to foreclosing on someone, but they must have known what they were getting into, and Smith never forgot that he was in business. Probably if he had forgot, he wouldn't have been trading for long."

Smith spends the better part of each nice day on the streets of Shelby Basin, the small market town just south of Clabberville. Sometimes he drops in to call on his sons, both of whom are merchants in town, but most often he just sits in his new red pickup truck, watches the girls, and waits for business to approach. The older citizens wave when they pass him; the younger workers more frequently march right by, perhaps because they don't know him, but more likely because their more modern temperament suggests another attitude toward this man of legendary wealth.

Five or six times in the course of the day, Smith will ease himself down from the truck. He does not carry himself with impressive vitality (I'm told he once did), but he is still sure of his step, and may the Lord grant me the same favor. He is a rangy, ruddy-faced, and big-boned man. Into his early eighties, as many amused citizens have commented, he was given to do his own building wrecking and his own carpentry. "I came by looking for work," says one young fellow, "and a voice from up in the rafters shouts out hello, and there's the old fellow peeling off tin roofing and sailing it down to the ground. And he said he didn't have anything for me."

Half a dozen times each day, when he clambers from the truck, he trods a stately course down the block to the Basin Coffee Shoppee. He orders chocolate milk every time. Every other visit he eats a dish of maple-walnut ice cream as well. While he eats he flirts with the waitress, and once I saw him get up in the middle of his sweet meal, buy four candy bars and hand them to the four little children sipping Cokes with their mother at a back table. "Say 'Thank you' to Mr. Smith, children," the mother said.

"He's an important contributor to the church in Clab-berville," says the lady whose late husband hunted with Smith. "He wanted to pay for the place to be painted once, but there was some sort of disagreement over the color or something. But he still gives a great deal. Not only that, but he's there every Sunday. And he always brings a big bag of candy. You should see the kids around him afterwards."

I approached the beast recommended by his long-time acquaintance and occasional traveling companion, Jimmy Barlow. I even brought along the rather complimentary pages I had written about Jimmy. OK, what did I want to know? And besides that, who did I work for, and where in town did I live, and oh, if I ever came to sell the farm, he'd buy the farm, as it was once a Smith homestead of some uncle of his.

He has always been a cagey one, and in his old age, his memory dimmed at opportune points. He's a hard man to talk to, but a charmer, nevertheless.

"How did you start in business?"

"I haven't stopped yet, and I started a while ago."

"Someone said you used to trade things from a wagon, that you'd buy a dozen chickens for fifty cents and sell them for a dollar."

"I might have. I did a little trading way back." Then he told me a fine story about another old trader, dead and gone a dozen years now. Excuse the digression, but the tale's the only thing he told me.

I shouldn't really say he "told" the story, because he did more than that—he sang it in short melodic assertions, each phrase rising, falling, and then suddenly cut off and punctuated with a fist slapped against the open palm, a hand swept through the air to show the size of whatever, a head nodding as if to release as a gift to the listener each item he listed. It is a special way of telling a story, a custom common to the older residents, who told tales when tales were fun to present and offered the principal entertainment of each day.

"Chester would trade anything, and he had a weekly wagon route. He'd trade a farmer his jackknife and trade that to another farmer at the next place. Well, one spring day someone wanted the horse from his wagon, so he unhitched it. The fellow put it in his barn, and gave three dollars for it. He promised to bring a bull down the next day to Chester's storehouse on Main Street besides. Well, the next day the fellow led a bull down Main Street all right. And it had been a good bull in its time, bred more than once to every cow on the farm, so it was a good animal at that. So good the fellow had kept it a few years more than he should have, until finally its hooves were grown up so high it was lame and it was so sick it couldn't eat, and owing to that, it was skinny enough so a man would think it had swallowed a bird cage.

"The fellow tied the bull in front of Chester's storehouse. All the men on the street saw the bull and they laughed and they said, 'Chester, if you've gone into the cattle trading business, that's a hell of a start.' Chester didn't say anything, and the matter passed, with folks thinking that for once someone had bested an old trader. Fact is, he butchered that bull the next day and gave the best part of it away for dog food.

"The whole summer went by with no more said, until it was time to cut corn. In those days, maybe twenty farmers would get together and do one man's corn patch, then move right on and do the next man's corn patch, and so on until everyone had their ensilage. Whichever farm they were at on a certain day, that man's wife had to make a big feed for all the men.

"Chester used to peddle fish, summers. He'd order a ton of whatever was cheapest from Boston—cod, scrod, haddock—used to say that a farmer didn't mind if it was a whale or a trout. Well, about the time the farmers were cutting corn up to the place where he had traded a good horse for a half-dead old bull, Chester came by with some fish.

" 'Have you got something good to feed all the men?'
says the lady of the house. 'I've got fish,' says Chester.
'No meat?' says the farmer's wife. 'Fish is OK, but the
men like meat after they've been working.' So Chester
showed them some good-looking steaks, just about the
right size so a man could eat a whole one, and the farmer's wife bought two dozen of them paid a pretty good
price for them too.

"Then he got on his wagon and went on down the
road, and at every house he stopped, did his business, and
then gave each lady a steak, telling each one just where
the meat had come from—the neck of the old bull he'd
butchered in the spring. I suppose those farmers ate quite
a few potatoes that night, because they couldn't have put
away much of that meat. Chester came out pretty close
to even in the end."

Fine for local color, but Smith had certainly not been
saying much about himself. "How did you make your
first million?" I asked.

"Never had much luck with first million, so I gave up
on it and started right in on the second," he said.

But what about the 13,000 acres I heard about in Florida, or the string of lumber mills down there, or the time
the Cuban customs officials took him from ship to a
hotel, guarded the door while he paced all night, and
booted him out of the country the next morning? What
about the deals in Costa Rica and in the Philippines?
Smith had very little to offer on those subjects. "I'm too
old to remember way back then," he said. Then he took
me in the Basin Coffee Shoppee and bought me a chocolate milk. That's all I can tell you and that's all I know.

The Medical Freak

I'VE MET ONE fanatic cat fan, a crazy old lady down in Shelby Basin who lives immersed in feline generations—a docile old pink grandma, like herself, draped above the head of her easy chair like a tiara, spotted working mothers perched like Egyptian statues on the arms of the chair, and ambitious young tigers batting about the laces of her black shoes. You can't chat with the old lady unless you want to hear about cats. She'll tell you where her son, a farmer friend of mine, might be working (which is why I know her). But that's about all she's good for. From then on it's, "Pinktoes never never goes outside when it's raining!" or, "Poor baby Sergeant, you had a nasty set-to with that shepherd from down the road, poor dear."

Bless the shepherd down the road, bless the hounds chained in Edgar Bradford's yard, bless Lady, Hank's amazing cow dog, and most of all bless Walter, a mean old critter with cats if there ever was one. Right-minded country people think of cats as rat catchers. A respectably self-employed family of cats makes its living full-time down at the dump.

I know a fellow who keeps ten cats in his barn and feeds them on the unmarketable clostrum milk of newly freshened cows. He's got one cat he can whistle up from anywhere. When she comes he has only to point to the crack in the floor where he has just seen a mouse disappear, and the cat will sit there, a half an hour if need be, frozen still, waiting for the varmint to show itself. Cats, by and large, are working animals, which, if left to their own devices, can easily fend for themselves.

Dogs are a different story. They address humans far more directly and their insistent personalities soon gain them special concessions from even the most hardhearted owners. The concessions are not always of the "Good Rover, here's a dog biscuit, you loyal pal" variety. What I mean to say is that dogs and masters work out complicated psychological "arrangements" so they can stand to be around each other day after day, for years on end.

Archie Plotnick's fat retriever, Max, is a different story. He is too dumb for any arrangements to be negotiable, so it's all one-sided—give, give, give on the part of Archie and his wife Yuni, and take take, take, take on the part of Max. Max will sit in his chair, even if Archie is sitting there already; and he will crouch staring, one paw up on the supper table, even after he has been told "No" quite sharply, and been given a smart rap upside the noggin.

Not so with Walter, the celebrated pig killer. Walter is about as smart as dogs come, which isn't all that smart, but is enough to eke out a meager living as a professional. After Walter killed my pigs, neighbors offered to shoot her for me, and I would have accepted but for some extenuating circumstances.

First, she was in the company of Aaron the killer

hound, who later took to attacking calves and had to be given to city people. Second, she was feeding eight puppies at the time, and that makes a dog all ravenous wild beast and no pet at all.

Instead, I asked Doc Mead to spay her, and she's been milder since. They say that dogs fatten up easily after they've been spayed, but Walter is still quite dapper. She leaves this year's pigs alone, but I believe she would have left Victoria and Albert alone too if she hadn't been influenced by Aaron and the puppies. About the only noticeable change in her habits is that she chases porcupines less.

Dogs lead two lives. That tends to surprise city friends who turn their charges loose up here for the first time. Curled up under the stove, Jacques or Pookie may appear to be the same old apartment hound, but turn him in the field, and Walter will soon revive his animal spirit, or run him ragged trying. After a few training expeditions to the spring or the stone wall up top of the mowing, the dogs will take to the woods, and not show again for a few hours. When they do reappear they will most likely be spattered with the gore of some late woodchuck or rabbit, or worse yet, will sport snouts full of hedgehog quills.

One of my neighbors jokes that he keeps a fine coon dog, best hunter he knows but that he's never seen a finer stickpig hunter than Walter. My own theory is that Walter is a medical freak. I know a girl like that in Brookline—she would rather be in the hospital than out and only seems to feel authentic and justified in keeping on living when she's locked up in the hospital with the doctors in attendance and the family in despair. As a result (or perhaps as a cause, to be fair) she spends a lot of time involved in major medical crises.

Walter is the same way. Last summer she came whimpering home no fewer than fifteen times, her nose, mouth, and paws bristling with long black-and-white quills. The local usage, "with her face like a pincushion," is no exaggeration of how a dog looks after attacking a porcupine.

Late one fall night last year, I caught a porcupine in the headlights just as I returned to the farm. Walter must have been watching from under the porch. I had stopped the car to avoid hitting the porcupine when I saw the poor fated mutt racing toward it. Her jaws were opened so wide and her gait so smooth and low that she made me think of an alligator, about to snap. She snapped and, without stopping, jumped a yard into the air. Then, howling in pain, she climbed through the open car window and sat trembling next to me.

Quills are legitimate medical crises. A quill is about the size of a darning needle, made out of plastic-like chitin, and barbed at its business end with microscopic rings. If a dog is lucky, she'll get off with a dozen or so in the nose. A mess of quills stuck into the roof of the mouth and tongue, and through the eyelids, can set a dog wild with panic and make breathing nearly impossible. I once lost a puppy to quills.

Standard practice here for severe cases is to tie the dog's front and back legs, jam its mouth open with a stick tied behind the ears, sit on the dog and go to work tugging at the quills with a pair of pliers.

Walter is not much of a struggler and I've never had to tie her. Like a true medical freak, she will slink up to me looking guilty for her foolishness, present the embellished snout, and sit whining in self-pity as I work tugging out the quills one after another. Following local advice, I've tried cutting the tips off the quills to "deflate them," and I've tried dabbing them with oil, both said to ease the extractions. I've yet to notice that either helps at all.

Walter is a constant instruction to me in the woods. She shows by her excited nosework where I can see the fresh tracks of a catamount. She shows by the sudden perking of her ears and cocking of her head where I can hear a deer cracking her course as she runs off, or where a rabbit has passed.

In the fields and about the house, she has clearly assigned me the role of leader of her pack and is awesomely sensitive to slight movements of arms and legs, or slight unconscious habits that signal a journey is in the making. In the woods the lure of dogly pursuits is too strong and she will ignore me and go her own way, try as I might to spare some rabbit and call her to heel.

More often than not, Walter will come back from these sylvan excursions stinking and stained with traces of some long rotted animal or its droppings. I wondered why until an old-timer pointed out to me that she has a fair share of terrier in her. "Those terriers will roll in manure every chance they get or whatever other rotten thing they can find. It masks their scent while they are hunting up animals."

I can picture a pair of rabbits sniffing the air as they trot through the woods. One rabbit says to the other, "We better hightail it out of here. Something's chasing us!" and the other rabbit says, "Aw, don't worry about it, it's only a manure out for its morning constitutional."

Walter is no vegetarian. Her steady diet is grumblies—the dried kibbled dog food that comes from the feed and grain store in fifty-pound sacks—supplemented with table scraps. She is healthy and energetic, but like a spoiled Jewish kid holding out on mother, she will not eat grumblies in front of me. I know she eats because I have to refill her bowl. Friends are amused to see her quivering with anticipation until humans are out of sight of her bowl.

One day last spring, when I was out of town, and no one else was here either, Bruce from down the road came up to feed Walter. He hardly had time to put down the bowl of grumblies before Walter was wolfing them down, right in front of him. Bruce feeds a dozen beef cows and is therefore in the habit of considering with care any sudden changes in an animal's eating habits. It's good he thought about it, because his wit saved his supper.

Walter had jumped into his car, extracted a wrapped package of pork chops from among the groceries on the back seat, and hidden the package in the tall grass behind the car. Then she set upon the grumblies to show she was an innocent dog. Bruce tramped around and located the chops; Walter left off eating the grumblies and crept under the porch.

My friend "the Tall Foreigner" made himself a rule a few years ago that he would not go anyplace his dog could not go, and he stayed out of the city for over a year out of consideration to Booger. Booger did not follow the same rules, however, and went off on his own, apparently where neither man nor beast should have trod, because he never came home, and "the Tall Foreigner" has again taken up travel.

One fellow who paid careful attention to dogs was Thomas Mann. His essay, "A Man and His Dog" (which may be found in the common Vintage paper edition of *Death in Venice*) is full of the sort of close observations of his own Bashan that leave me feeling imprudent for daring to write about dogs at all.

Neighbors

New England wasn't designed for recluses, freaks, or "new-age farmers." It was designed for neighbors who liked to visit each other in the long winters, and who set up housekeeping long before cars and snowplows made the proverbial winding tree-lined driveway possible. It's common to travel miles down country lanes, passing hundreds of acres of woods and fields on both sides, only to arrive at a crossroads with four farmhouses set so close together you might think land was scarce.

So it is that high atop the hill one may find not one but two houses, two barns, two chicken coops, situated so that all concerned can go about their daily chores confident that they won't miss a thing. The neighbors, as long as they were here, shared all our troubles, all our joys, and dull Tuesday afternoons. Their visitors were our visitors and their deliverymen, our deliverymen. Yet it was a rare month when we would speak to each other twice.

The hill is a place of unusual distinction. A monument deep in the woods commemorates the site of "the first schoolhouse in America to fly an American flag." On that sacred slope, the Gurneys assure me, their farm was "the first place north of the monument built of vertical slab siding"—the first not hewn of logs but built of lumber hauled to and from the sawmill. Their house was joined by about thirty other dwellings—cabins, huts, one improved cave, and a general store, which are now marked only by occasional cellar holes and stone walls in the woods. Only three places have endured. Theirs had already stood a century when the Gurneys bought it from relatives forty-three years ago. Old Brad farmed it until about 1963, when a series of heart attacks forced him to sell off his stock. He grew progressively weaker, and died a few years ago, about two years after I first came to the hill.

During the six years of his illness, Mrs. Gurney took over the garden and chickens. For a while she kept one cow, which she milked by hand. She shoveled clear paths all winter and once got herself stuck in a hole in the crust of the snow for an hour before Brad noticed and summoned help. She also mowed the lawn near the house all summer.

People in town here, whom you would not mistake for city slickers, used to call the Gurneys "hicks." The Gurneys always found a way to live away from others. Although TV made them somewhat world-wise in old age, they seldom went to town even in their working days. Aside from their family, the Gurneys' only friends were the folks who used to live in our house. From what I gather, though, they never went so far as to share chores or equipment or necessary but seldom used stock, such as a bull or a boar.

I write about them here because they bewilder me, because they seem more real on the page than they ever did out the window. I have often wondered what they thought and what they saw when they watched the comings and goings here. They always maintained the strictest distance, refusing to be enticed by friendliness, gossip, or the seeking of their advice. The good pastor who sold me the house mentioned them once.

"The Gurneys will be no trouble to you," he said. "They are very private people."

Never Sign a Paper for a Stranger.

Summers, a dense growth of leaves hides their house completely from view, and some days you forget it is there. But come first frost, the leaves fall and the houses are again exposed. Then, I would feel as public as they did private. What secrets could they have had, these old folk, but the times they took their pills and their choice of TV programs?

I will recount in nearly its entirety the history of our dealings together. And you may end up as puzzled by them as I am.

When we moved in, their world must have changed. I hadn't been in the house a month when we received a notice that a motorcycle rally would pass up the hill road heading into the woods. I got all excited and invited thirty or so friends from other farms in the area to come have breakfast and watch the show.

Things went well enough until the first bike roared

past. Then, like a fast caterpillar, all thirty freaks dashed out to the roadside, making a stand right across from the Gurneys' front window. You could see them in there, pointing to that fellow's long beard, that girl's yellow robes, pointing and nodding like they were discussing a picture in a magazine and not real live human beings who were peeping shyly back at them.

Soon after that, I offered to plow their garden for them, just for the practice. Mrs. Gurney named day and hour, I came and did my work and refused payment. She was a bit disturbed when I rolled over her strawberry bed, which I hadn't noticed for the weeds already rising in it. Later that summer, she mentioned to me that she guessed I hadn't done her plants any harm and offered to sell me some strawberries. Sell? After I had spent hours plowing for her and hadn't harmed her plants? After that I brought her some melons and some peas. She thanked me and took them.

Late that fall, as we worked digging up potatoes, I heard again and again, a light clink, clink, clink, the sound of metal striking metal, barely discernible across the road. Eventually I went to see what it was, and discovered the Gurneys working together in their woodshed. Brad, for all his frailty, would place the ax blade gently on a thin slab of wood, and Mrs. Gurney would haul the five-pound sledge up a foot into the air by its head, and let it fall onto the ax. At this rate it would have taken them until summer to split their day's stove wood. I offered to help out, and Mrs. Gurney said, "You can try."

I did try. For six weeks I would go over there and spend a few hours splitting a week's wood. It is not always easy to find enjoyable physical tasks like that, and I do not think I begrudged them a swat of it. I thought I detected a slight thaw in their cautious attitude. He might greet me and say they "sure were glad to have the wood split" the other morning when it was twenty below.

Then one day we had seven loaves of bread risen and just placed in the oven when we ran out of cooking gas. I called up Mrs. Gurney and she said to bring them over. When I came she said, "I guess you done enough work so we owe this to you." Later, when I returned to pick up the loaves, I found she hadn't taken them out of the bread pans to cool, so they were all soggy.

Toward spring, I left the farm one night at about eleven. The Gurneys' house was dark, but just on a whim, I waved at its shadow. Next day when I went to split wood, I said to Mrs. Gurney, "Did you notice when I waved to you last night?"

"I was wonderin' how you seen me," said Mrs. Gurney. "I was standin' so far back!"

I should have been pleased that I was blessed with neighbors who "look but don't touch." After all, things could easily have been worse. After Brad passed away she sold the place to city folk who use it as a weekend snowmobile clubhouse.

THINK TWICE BEFORE YOU
SUE YOUR NEIGHBOR.

A Dollar a Boid a Year

Nicholas Nozzle, for seventeen years janitor and handyman at a glue factory on Long Island, talked things over with the wife, his old man, her old man, and next thing you know he'd signed a chicken contract and packed his bags and taken the big step. Nick has an uncommon interest in the horse track and got on the inside by breeding a few so-so nags of his own. It was a friend at the track who had passed him the lowdown about chicken contracts.

"A dollar a boid a year," said Nick, "that's what we expect to make when the market is down. When it's good they got all kinds of bonuses and extra percentage allowances, so it can come to a pretty good deal, if you're lucky."

The history of American agriculture has many a sordid chapter. One of the obviously inevitable but nevertheless saddening tales concerns the promise and failure of agricultural cooperatives. What could be more obvious than for farmers to group together to command the lowest possible prices on truckloads of fertilizer and feed grain, large orders of equipment, bulk seed purchases, megatons of dread pesticide?

As might be expected, Jewish egg farmers in the Catskills have set themselves up a buying cooperative that really works for them. Most were city merchants who moved out during the Depression. Many were businessmen before they were farmers, and the knowledge has stood them in good stead. Hardy, occasionally foolhardy Yankee farmers have seldom been able to perpetuate such cooperatives. Whenever cooperatives in New England have become well established, they have evolved into regular retail operations. Nowadays, the universal practice is to buy from regional grain suppliers —only three or four biggies survive of an earlier proliferation—and they are owned, of course, by huge national corporations.

Last year, after I spent $400 for lime to sweeten hayfields (the government paid half of it back to me) and paid my bill promptly, I let a small subsequent bill for half a dozen sacks of grain slide for a month. Second bill they sent had eighteen percent interest tacked on, the dirty work done by some computer. So I learned the friendly neighborhood feed store was only a wishful illusion.

Well, this same outfit that charged me eighteen percent interest on six sacks of grain put Nicholas Nozzle into the egg business by offering him the chicken contract.

Fancy this: here's this big company—one of the ones which necessitated the coining of the common farm language "agribusiness." They will sell you horse feed, horse blankets, horsefly powder, they will sell you a hoof knife to trim the hooves of a horse, they will sell you a stainless, seamless milk pail to milk a goat, a milk parlor if you have a hundred cows to milk, a system of automatic watering troughs for thirsty chickens, a snow blower to keep the way to the barn clear, a tractor and wagon to haul hay up the cleared way to the barn, a freezer to keep this year's home beef in, a well-drilling contract to keep all the troughs, piping, sinks, pails, pumps, sumps, traps, and drains they will sell to you gushing with water. Nominally, they are a still a co-operative, returning a proportion of yearly receipts to each farmer who owns shares. I asked a few farmers and no one knew what they'd gotten back: "Not so many dollars as might make me recall the amount."

This agribusiness made a deal with Nicholas Nozzle, converting him from janitor and horse breeder into farmer. The agribusiness supplies chickens galore, of laying age (about six months). They supply grain to feed the chickens, and if necessary, they supply veterinary services. Nicholas supplies building and equipment, labor, and electricity. That's a chicken contract.

The agribusiness owns all the eggs the chickens lay. They pick up the crates of eggs at the farm, sort, wash, and market them as they see fit, and they return to Nicholas about fifteen percent (depending on the market). Nicholas grossed a little better than a dollar a boid last year. He keeps thirteen thousand chickens at a time, tends them six to eight hours a day.

Really, it can hardly be called farming at all. It is more a continuation of janitorial services. All the work is indoors, in one long, gray concrete blockhouse sixty feet wide and sixty yards long. "The building's all wrong," says Nick. "It should only be forty feet wide, so the center could get cool enough. As it is the boids in the center rows are always a little too hot, and it shows in their production. Also, there are some center posts here and there, and they get in the way of the automatic grain cart, so we have to feed about a thousand boids by hand. That takes time. But all in all, we're in here a regular working day, cleaning up, gathering twice a day, feeding.

"If I had the money," Nicholas continued, "I'd build some more housing and tell them to put in some more chickens. What I'd really like is this design they got, forty feet wide and three hundred and sixty-three feet long, holds thirty thousand boids. Get one of them and you can make a buck—costs one hundred and fifty Gs to put up though."

And while Nicholas talked to me, I stared at the multitude of chickens, all yelling and beating their wings against the sides of their cages for fear of the new being who had come into their quarters. It didn't look any too healthy to me. The chickens are in wire cages twenty-eight inches square on the floor, and about a foot high. They are kept four to a cage, giving each animal about fifty square inches of living room. (Old free chickens used to get about five square feet apiece.) The cages are stacked in banks, clear up to the ceiling.

"Before I got this place, a guy used to leave chickens free in here. He could only fit in four thousand and had problems with smothering and plus he had to clean up after them," said Nick. Smothering happens when loose birds panic and head for the nearest corner. They will walk over or settle on whatever is there already, so the first birds to reach the corner suffer. Wire cages do away with this problem. They also stop crowding and fighting among birds, because the groups of four are too small to have a pecking order that will make any difference.

An automatic cart pumps feed into the troughs as Nick drives it down the long corridors of cages. Watering is automatic. And chicken shit (one hundred and twenty-five pounds a year from each bird) falls through the floor of the cages into a sunken gutter, whence electric scrapers mounted on a moving cable force it along and finally shove it out a port at the end of the building and into the waiting trucks of neighboring farmers. Because the cage floors are sloped, when a chicken lays an egg, it rolls outside the cage, coming to rest on a shelf from which Nick can retrieve it quickly. Almost no breakage occurs.

The agribusiness chickens are about the worst-looking animals I've ever seen. They are almost all half bald, ragged, and listless. "How come the chickens are half bald?" I asked Nick.

"It's a good sign," he said, "because it shows they're eating and laying. They scrape feathers off reaching out of the cages after food, and besides, a boid should be growing eggs, not feathers. What does she want with feathers here? It's cold?" I wondered if bald cows might give more milk.

The chickens are pushed for all the production possible. They lay, on the average, one egg every day and three quarters, one egg every forty-two hours, maybe two hundred and fifty eggs a year. When they first arrive, their eggs are small, but they soon produce mediums, and late in their short lives, most are laying large eggs. If they were family hens, they would be allowed

116

to loiter throughout the winter, molting, and perhaps offering an egg once every few weeks. Come spring, they'd start laying again, small at first (but larger than the first cycle), and jumbo toward fall. No dice. The birds of agribusiness are shipped out as soon as their first production cycle flags, sold as a group to Campbell's for chicken soup. The chicken house is "sanitized" and a new flock of layers is installed.

The Lord preserve us from that soup. The chicken grain contains corn, alfalfa, wheat, bone meal, and soybeans. It also contains the most God-awful selection of medications and laying stimulants, including two hormones, methionine hydroxy analogue and deactivated animal sterol (at least that's what the local doctor says they are), which I would sooner not eat. The feed is called "Nu-Munnygrower."

I kept chickens here in Clabberville all one summer, and it's easy to see how they have come to be mistreated. They are the most unresponsive, dumb, and noisy creatures harbored by man. I kept four, and they would take to rotating counterclockwise whenever I entered their pen, trying to stay as far from me as possible. They never learned at what hour I fed them. It took them a day to discover their water, in fact.

When they were good, they were very bountiful indeed, laying an egg a day apiece throughout the month of August. By October they were arguing about which one of them would give this week's egg. The first of November I gave them away to friends who ate them come Thanksgiving.

Chickens are disturbingly alien beings. If a chicken were, say, my fourth cousin, twice removed by marriage, a cow would be my twin brother on the same scale. They are utterly beyond understanding, more like

117

insects than like warm-blooded animals. They move here and there without apparent reason, stop dead still, turn and eye some rock or wall for a minute, scream, and wander off to undertake other unfathomable pursuits.

Chickens have one constant habit, one endearing grace that seems an atoll of consistency in an ocean of senseless clucking. Hens make a nice burbling sound when they lay eggs. Robert Herrick, who took passing notice of several of the world's strange beings, ennobled this noise with his verse:

> A hen
> I keep which creeking day by day,
> Tells when
> She goes her long white egg to lay.

I like Herrick, who points out one of the animal's few pleasant traits, but I don't like chickens much, nevertheless. Poor Nicholas Nozzle who has to spend all day with them. Poor consumers who find Nick's ugly agribusiness boids in their soup.

When Winter Comes

IT'S A TRAIT you need not notice until you leave the city. I'm just catching on now. People in the country move with the seasons, just like the birds, the bees and, of course, the bears. Most of all like the bears.

An air of frenzy surrounds the final chores of fall on the farm—chinking up the north wall of the cow shed to keep out the coming icy wind, moving the fencing back where it won't be crushed by the snow-plow that plunges by after each storm, the hopeful attempt between thunderstorms in early November to squeeze a third cutting of hay from choice fields.

Then, in one of those miracles of sudden transition which Mother Nature offers up, the air gusts strong one day, then turns suddenly still. Hank the dairy farmer says to me, "We're gonna have some winter tonight, I guess," and rushes to rewire the heat lamps which keep his milk house plumbing thawed.

The next morning, all the plants in all the gardens in the valley have keeled over and died. My neighbor Harold Toy drops by with a bushel of tomatoes. His farm is high on the side of a mountain. As hot air rises when the cold pours into the valleys, sidehill farms such as his generally have a growing season which lasts a few days or a week longer. "It's probably going to frost at our place tonight," he says, "and Ruth insists she's not going to can another tomato, so you people take these."

I might be in our own garden at the time, prodding the wilted lettuce with my toe, looking for a few sheltered morsels that have survived. The broad leaves of the winter squash (it will keep all winter in a cool basement) have suddenly shriveled, uncovering half a dozen small fruits missed in the last hasty picking. They are too bruised to keep, but are OK if we eat them right away.

We spend a final frenetic few days, working in the now bitter chill. Hank wants a hand maneuvering all the machinery into the long dark storage shed. In go the baler, the grass chopper, the corn rig, the tedder, the cultivator, the conditioner, and the yellow truck. The ground freezes rock hard and we are able to get a jeep into the woods on a road usually too sodden with glut of full underground springs to be passable. We haul out an extra two cords of wood, cut earlier and left in the hope we'd have such a freeze before snow.

Then snow. A few flakes one dusk in mid-December, and the next morning no more garden, no more grass, no more road out to the real world. Each winter comes this way, and everybody is astonished all over again. Even the old lady down the road, who has never in all her seventy-eight years been anywhere else when the first snow hit town, even she says, "Sure came on us sudden, that snow."

It did, too. I go into a sort of shock as the size of the available world diminishes. It's a touch of claustrophobia; I walk about stoop-necked. I suspect, in the manner of the well-trained intelligentsia, that it's my private problem, and that other people are feeling just fine. But of course that's not true. Some robust portion of every person's soul staggers off like a bear on ice, curls up with knees pressed hard against chin, and cringes in sleep until spring.

Can you determine the one moment when water begins to boil? Of course there is no such moment; either it's not boiling or it has started already. In nether suburbia where I grew up, perhaps a whole month was taken up with wishy-washy quasi-winter—some snow, then sun, a bit of rain, a ghostly warm day, and slowly winter would ease in on us.

Up here, it snows for four days straight, and seemingly a scant week out of summer, it's deep winter. It could be March, to look out the window; September, October, November, March. But it is only December, and the prospect of months to come has few consolations. One is winter sports, although I stay clear of ski-land.

Snowshoeing is sport only in the sense that walking is, because it's not much different from walking. Here's the entry from my diary for Tuesday, January 27, of a recent winter: "Snowshoed up to the power line. The falls, iced over and then blanketed with snow, is hardly noticeable—one would have to know it was there in order to find it. Walter ran ahead, obscuring the tracks of showshoe hares, though I didn't get a good look at the tracks before she did her work. And as far as I could go, always snowmobile sounds."

I am not sure of the effect of snowmobiles, and they are probably too newly abundant for much to be known, but I suspect they constitute one more great ecological tragedy. More and more New England farmland has gone back to woods in the past several decades and with the accompanying copious browse which grows up in abandoned pastures, things looked good for animals for a time. A peculiar balance-of-power was struck, with man replacing bear and puma as chief predator, and several common small animals with valuable pelts missing altogether. The snowmobile may change all that.

Where no man and few animals traveled for half the

year, major turnpikes now penetrate the woods. Here, on the hill, a week might pass in summer without a stranger driving up the road. But on any winter weekend morning, twenty or thirty rearing, fuming snowmobiles will careen past, usually in packs of five or six.

Now there is no easy changing of the seemingly inexorable self-degradation of America. If it is slowed in one place, her imaginative captains of industry will discover another route over the cliff. Let me not blame the crowds of weekenders who enjoy sitting astride these stinking, roaring engines on treadmills and chasing the Joneses through the wilderness. Most are peaceable, law-abiding folks who would be astonished and incredulous to hear that their fun has harmful consequences.

Here's what happens in the woods because of the snowmobiles: wherever they go—and they go everywhere—they leave trails hard enough to walk on. That sets the scene. Then some winter sportsmen (the rotten apples, no doubt) go charging through deer yards, the little areas of trampled snow far from houses and roads where the deer huddle together for the months when the snow is too deep to allow travel.

Storming of the deer yards forces the panicked animals, slow and weak because of the scarcity of food, to take to the woods, struggling through the deep snow in exhausting leaps. Then come the dogs, ordinary towsers and rovers, everybody's summertime pals reminding us that they have an animal life of their own. The dogs, like the snowmobilers, travel in packs up the trails, penetrating far into the woods, where they never would have ventured at all had not men packed hard trails for them. Despite town laws requiring the chaining of dogs during the season of deep snow, the packs form, and kills are frequent—though hardly approaching the carnage the sportsmen vent a month or two earlier.

The dogs kill by "running deer" until they are exhausted. The deer are then hamstrung, and lie abandoned until found by shocked passersby. "They didn't even kill to eat the poor thing," says the sentimental sportsman, separating his own motives from those of beasts. Dogs do kill to eat, by the way, but they are carrion eaters, and like to let matters cool off for a time. They drop by now and then for a snack.

The sportsmen experience great emotional outrage about the dogs, and about the owners who let their pets loose to run. Some pack pistols on their snowmobile jaunts, and every year some favorite pets are shot for following where neither sportsmen nor dogs belong, where even an itinerant snowshoer like me ought to tread softly.

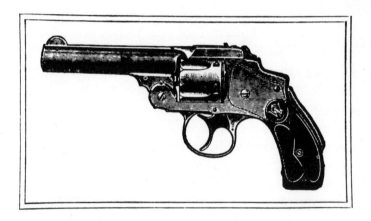

Sugaring

THERE'S AN OLD FARMER in the next town whose name is Hubert. Last year Hubert retired, married his housekeeper ("I don't have to pay her salary that way," he joked), sold his farm, and bought a small "all-electric" house down the road in which to pass his golden years.

Before Hubert retired, his farm was an anachronism doggedly surviving. He was milking eight cows when he quit—actually seven and a half because one had stepped on her back teats and was only being milked from the front quarters—and had never milked more than ten when he was running full blast. That's not enough cows to make a living nowadays, and probably hasn't been since the Depression. I don't think there's anyone left now bothering with even twice as many.

In fact Hubert made only part of his living selling milk. He also drove a school bus, taking an hour after morning chores and an hour before evening chores to cart eight neighbors' children to and from the regional school. This job is commonly a pensioner's plum, given by the town fathers to some respected citizen who is paid a fixed fee in return for hauling the kids in his own car.

There's no question that Hubert fit into the respected citizen category. For as many years as he wished the job, he was the judge at the local fall fair for all manner of horse-drawing contests. He still carries a reputation as a first-rate plowman, won in the days when horses were used for farm work. His barn was always freshly white-washed, his empty grain sacks folded and stored in numbered bundles, his mangers never showed the matted signs of yesterday's feed. He kept his barn like he was a fussy old widower—which, now that I mention it, is just what he was.

The few cows and the school bus route might have brought in enough for meager survival, but Hubert's pride, favorite work, and most concentrated source of capital was his sugarbush, and it was one of the best in the area.

A sugarbush is a tended stand of sugar maple trees. Hubert's was well thinned, with an eye for eliminating competing varieties, diseased trees, and overly dense clusters. The best stands have been producing for generations; it is the sort of thing a man works at now and then for the good of his grandchildren.

You may drive through this area of the country and not see these beautiful stands, because likely as not they are located on a side hill in the deep woods behind the farm and are accessible only by horse, crawler tractor, snowmobile or, lest we forget, by foot. You will see other signs, however, which will let you know you are in sugar country. Along the road frontage of the older farms you may frequently see stalwart ranks of maples. They are there not only because of their grandeur, but because trees along the road are easily accessible in deep snow.

Another sign is the sugarhouses. Some of the older ones are stone or brick, with massive chimneys reaching above their single room. Hubert's sugarhouse, like most around here, was a weathered board shack. Were he to take you inside, you would find a great oak cask which stores four or five barrels of sap after it is collected from the trees. The cask, made over fifty years ago, by the last cooper in town, was suspended high on the uphill end of the sugarhouse. In its bung was a spout leading into a long boiling pan with a deeply corrugated bottom. A wood furnace, called an "arch," was built in under the pan. It fed on a great stack of wood stored in the adjoining woodshed.

Hubert's method changed in only one material respect during his forty-five years of sugaring. Sometime in the early fifties, he doesn't remember just when, he turned Old Dobbin out to pasture for the last time and bought a crawler tractor. In all other respects his work remained the same, season after season, and the marks of each year's production may still be seen scratched inside the door of the sugarhouse cupboard.

About the first of March, Hubert would go around on the crawler "setting taps." Once a tedious job done with auger and a special mallet, small gasoline-powered drills now make it light work. A tree a foot and a half in diameter will have, say, two taps set into it on opposite sides. A hole is drilled through the bark and the tap inserted— it has a short bit of pipe which sticks into the tree and a spout and bucket hook which stick out. A tree a yard wide might take six or seven taps. They say that as long as you don't tap the same spot twice in a row, the practice does the tree no harm.

During the setting of taps the only unhealthy, modern, unorganic, and poisonous part of the process sometimes takes place. Little pellets of paraformaldehyde are placed in the hole in the tree before the tap is inserted. Their purpose is to keep the hole from sealing over and to "prevent the sap from going sour on you." One is cautioned not to drink the sap until it has been boiled, once it has passed over these pellets. Hubert says, "You can forget them pellets, and things work just about the same. I tried it both ways fine." In the last year or two, fewer farmers have been using the pellets, chiefly because the tapped holes don't heal as quickly after the season is finished, and some trees have been damaged or lost from rot.

About the tenth of March of Hubert's last sugaring season, I got a call from Hubert's housekeeper—not yet his wife. "This is Hubert's housekeeper," she said to me, "and he asked me to call you."

Hubert's voice: "You the one works for Hank?" I allow that I do sometimes, but not too often. "You're the one. You drive a crawler?" I learned to drive a crawler. It's very easy—like a tractor except that it's steered with brake levers for each track, and not with a wheel.

Sugaring is nice work because it is frequently done on the nicest spring days. If there's a cold sleety day, stay home because the sap is probably barely running anyway. When a day of forty-five or fifty follows on the heels of a cold night, the sap drips into the bucket so fast "it almost comes in a stream." If there is a string of days like this, the buckets will want emptying about every twenty-four hours.

Maybe fifteen times during the season, I got a call from Hubert's housekeeper. No introduction. The phone would ring about seven in the morning, and she'd be there, "Sap's running. Hubert says come down."

I'd go and the crawler would be waiting, a sled hitched behind it bearing a collecting vat. I'd drive into the woods, first with Hubert along to teach me the routes, and later by myself. Every five or ten trees I'd stop and slog through the mushy deep snow, dump the buckets into larger "collecting pails," and, after wading back to the crawler, dump these in turn into the collecting vat. After a few hundred buckets, the vat would be full, and, maneuvering over rotten logs and through snowdrifts, I'd draw it back to the sugarhouse and dump the sap into the collection barrel, running it in through a length of gutter pipe adapted for the purpose.

Meanwhile, Hubert had fired up the evaporator and started boiling off. I'd go in to visit for a moment before returning to my soggy labors. The sweet steam would billow all about the sugarhouse, rising out through slats in the eaves. Hubert would be stooped over, his face bright red as he stuffed wood into the furnace. Then he'd rush around to the final chamber in the big evaporating pan and test the syrup with a flat wooden spoon. As long as the syrup runs off the edge in drops, it is still too thin. When it begins to drip sluggishly off in chisel-shaped slabs, the final chamber in the pan can be emptied, and new syrup allowed to flow in.

Hubert waved a finger toward the frothing brown syrup. "See over here, Mark. I've got a chunk of salt pork wired an inch over the syrup. You know why? No, of course you don't know why. That's so if the syrup starts to boil over, it hits the pork and melts a little over the surface. Puts the froth right down again nice where it belongs."

As you might have suspected, things aren't like that anymore. There is still a fellow over in Shelby Basin whose collecting sled is horse-drawn. But for the most part, even the crawler tractor is outmoded, and the big oak barrel suspended over the wood-fired evaporator is an antique. Nowadays, taps are set from a snowmobile—about the only honest use of those devilish contraptions in New England. The taps are joined in a great web by pipeline, and the pipelines run from tree to tree through the sugarbush, and perhaps down through a mile of plain old woods to a galvanized collection tank set up for the season by the side of a road. You can see them if you drive through the area in March. The sap is picked up by truck for a local commercial sugarhouse. The big tourist-oriented sugarhouses buy raw sap from whomever will sell to them—and more and more farmers are confining their sugaring operations to "setting pipe" and letting the sugarhouses worry about the rest. When the sap arrives from the truck, it goes into a huge stainless-steel vat, thence into sanitary oil-fired boilers where its density is read by hydrometers (no more wooden spoon with chisel-shaped drops), and finally on to the automatic can filler.

The price of a gallon of maple syrup, bought straight from a small farmer, has risen in the past year from $6.50 to about $9. If you stop at one of the commercial sugarhouses along the Mohawk Trail or Route 9 in Vermont you're more likely to pay still another few dollars. If you can find a place that has various grades, the heavier grades (sugar is rated Fancy, A, B, C, and D) are both cheaper and tastier. Modern production methods allow more of the highest, clearest stuff, of assuringly uniform quality, to be produced than in any previous time.

It takes about thirty-two gallons of sap to make a gallon of syrup. The year I worked for Hubert he set one thousand buckets—about all that can be handled by a man and a boy who have other jobs to do as well. In the course of the month, Hubert made three hundred and thirty-five gallons of syrup, down a score or so from the year before. He sold it to a girl's prep school in Vermont for $6.50 a gallon. I thought the school was very nice to shell out $2,177.50 for maple syrup to keep the girls happy. I got paid one leather flight jacket, left over from the last world war, four gallons of syrup, one hauling chain, and about $10 cash. This year Hubert's sugarbush was left untapped. Now I hear that the new owner, a professor from New York, has hired it out for next season to one of the big sugarhouses.

Cow Practice

CALL YOUNG DOC MEAD. He's a real old-time Yankee," said Farmer Jones.

So I call young Doc Mead and tell him I want to ride around with a vet doing dairy practice, and that I'd heard he would be the most likely person to ask.

"Yes, I suppose I am the most likely," he says, and the next day we are off before eight, to make stallside visits to sick cows.

Doc Mead seems almost too good to be true. The tall, dark, and handsome son of a farmer still milking thirty cows, Doc went off to college in the Midwest. "I didn't intend to become a vet, but I looked around and that's where I ended up. I wanted to be outside a lot, wanted to do something that presented a challenge, and didn't want to get too far away from farming."

He drives a cranky green Ford pickup, which brings us to Mel Carter's farm about seven fifty, just as Mel finishes morning milking. He's got one cow with a high fever, off feed, down in her milk production, listless except for a wince when her stomach is prodded. "I gave her a magnet, seemed to help some," says Mel. Cows sometimes eat pieces of barbed wire, nails, old fencing staples, and such parts of tractors and bailers as come loose in the fields and get snarled up in their hay. You take a magnet about the size of a small cake of soap, and, with a tool that places the offering deep in the throat, force the cow to swallow it. (The vet first uses a pocket compass to tell if she already has a magnet.) It settles in the second stomach, and attracts the hardware collection, slowly drawing out the barbed wire from the stomach wall. Elevating the front of the cow five or six inches by putting a sack of sand under the front feet also helps, and if all goes well, in about two weeks the irritation to the stomach will have ceased, and the cow will milk well again.

I thought Mel's herd was fantastic. He wasn't milking many more than twenty cows, but he had beautiful registered Holsteins, their names and records printed on slates hung over each stanchion. I'd guess his herd averaged about seventeen thousand pounds of milk a year per cow. Big factory farmers, milking several hundred cows in loose housing and parlor, are happy with a thirteen-thousand-pound average, which is also about the national average at this point.

Mel had cows milking twenty thousand pounds—championship stuff. Yet he milks in an old wood-floored stable—with so few cows he can't afford a new concrete-floored barn. Although the barn is immaculate, the state threatens to close him down if he doesn't modernize. His equipment and labor costs are partially defrayed by the sharing of equipment and help with his brother, who runs a large orchard next door. Mel is a college graduate and has been running his farm for about thirty years—not what you expect to meet milking a few cows at the end of some back road.

Doc Mead next turned to the chore that brings him to Mel's farm once a month—pregnancy testing. He donned a long rubber glove that flared out at the top to envelop his left shoulder as well. The hand and arm disappeared into one cow after another, and cowshit slopped out, displaced by his arm. "This one's open," he said about the first cow. That means the first attempt at artificial insemination was not successful and the cow will require a "second service."

A cow is usually milked for ten months and "dried off" for about two months, after which she calves and starts giving milk again. Of course she'll have a hard time calving if she hasn't been pregnant, so at the end of her second month of giving milk, she will be "bred back." It's quite a trick to get a cow bred properly. She'll come into heat about every twenty-one days, and be fertile for less than twenty-four hours. It takes a sharp eye and experience to spot the heat early enough so the "A. I. man" can be summoned and the cow serviced.

Frequently two or three services are necessary before a cow is successfully bred. Not only is this costly, but in terms of the cow's lifetime production, multiple servicing means considerable loss of salable milk. When a cow stays open an extra month, she will consume thirteen months' worth of food and grain to give twelve months' worth of milk, require feeding and cleaning work for the month, and be a source of irritation besides.

So one of the best investments a farmer can make, and one which reflects the changing nature of veterinary practice, is a regular pregnancy inspection by the vet. It

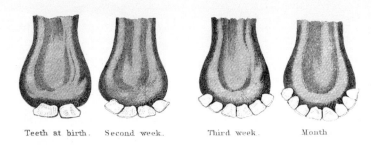

Teeth at birth. Second week. Third week. Month

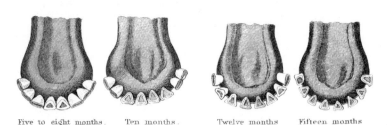

Five to eight months. Ten months. Twelve months Fifteen months

TEETH AT DIFFERENT AGES.

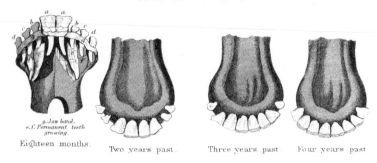

g. Jaw band.
e.f. Permanent teeth
growing.

Eighteen months. Two years past. Three years past Four years past

is in the nature of procedural medicine, as opposed to the do-or-die ambulance calls which used to characterize a rural practice.

Doc Mead examined three cows and found two pregnant, and the open one healthy and able to be fertilized. On the way out of the farm we chatted for a few minutes with Mel's wife and gave her four vials of vaccine

136

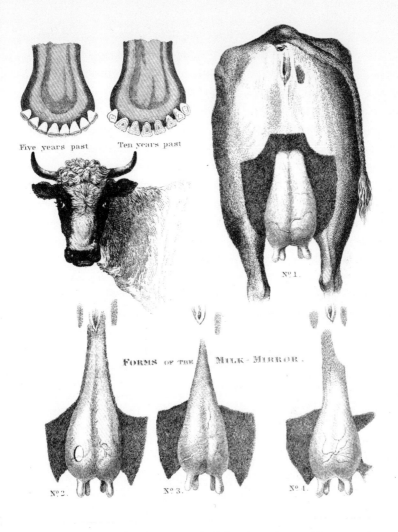

Five years past   Ten years past

FORMS OF THE MILK-MIRROR.

Nº 1.

Nº 2.   Nº 3.   Nº 4.

against the equine encephalitis that is causing panic among southern horse owners. She planned to administer them herself, so Doc Mead charged her only a nominal fee for the medicine.

We rode half an hour east, finally came to the big dairy factory owned by the Wanowski brothers. Their land used to be prime shade-tobacco fields, but the demand for Connecticut River Valley tobacco has gone down in recent years, and the fields have been turned to the less lucrative production of food for milk cows.

"Here's where you learn that farming isn't declining, Mark," says the doc. "The number of farmers is going way down, but there aren't any fewer cows than there ever were. It used to be there were ten farmers in a row and they didn't have a hundred cows between them. Now you come here to this one place and there are three hundred." It may be true, although the milk-truck driver says he is picking up less milk than ever before. Anyway, Doc Mead was speaking merely about the number of cows, while answering my lament for a passing way of life.

I would like to have seen the face of Doc Mead's great-grandfather, if he had been able to drive into the barnyard with us. Five different pieces of heavy equipment were in operation—a grain hopper truck blowing feed into a grain loft, a road-building sized bucket loader scooping up silage, a cement mixer churning around mix for the floor of a huge new barn and feed lot, a small scraper-tractor shoving manure out of the walkway of a barn, and a hay baler and thrower raking through the field adjacent to the barnyard.

"Cows here don't get the individual attention they do over at Mel's place. They cause too much trouble and out they go. And we don't see them until their sickness has gone further along. Chances are the herdsman treats most of his own sickness—you get a herd this size and pretty soon you have experienced everything. So we are only called on the sticky cases, where he has tried what he knows, is still in trouble, and thinks it's worth paying me."

First Doc Mead examined about twenty cows for pregnancy, one after the other. One had not conceived in four services. "Beef her," said the older and taller Wanowski. Three needed treatment for cystic growths preventing conception. One cow was in heat right when examined, and nobody had noticed. "In these big places the cows have numbers and not names. They feed in a common area and they are run through the parlor twice a day for milking. It's easy to miss trouble that would be obvious to a small farmer who knows each cow by name."

Doc Mead's findings were entered on a print-out sheet from a computer. It contained records of every cow, her previous services, production, profit over feed cost, variation from the national average for her breed, and a few other items which might influence a decision about whether to cull or keep the animal.

After the testing, Doc was taken to the hospital and shown three sick cows. One had an infected foot which had dropped her milk production. "It started with a nail puncture, through which dirt keeps introducing infection. I can shave the hoof material and clean it up, and control the infection with medication, but the original wound will keep filling up again and again. The cow is not out of production yet, but you'll lose money if you breed her back again." While he said this, he was paring away with a special hoof knife, while one Wanowski brother held the foreleg up and another restrained her by means of a halter fastened around the scoop of the front end loader. The cow shuddered and groaned with fear.

"Cows in a stanchion barn are used to being handled. You can treat them easily. In loose housing, except for milking, a cow can go for months without being touched. It keeps them skittish."

Before leaving the Wanowski farm we stopped to inoculate the horse belonging to the hired man's daughter. She had just won an award at a cattle show for the best Brown Swiss. "Grand Champion, that's what it was for," said her ma. We admired the ribbon.

Final stop for the morning was at the farm of old Henry, seventy-two, still milking fifteen cows. A cow had just freshened the night before but had not completely expelled the afterbirth. She was out in the pasture, grazing with the others, and did not seem particularly bothered by the mess of innards hanging alongside her tail. "They'll start to let down milk and if you don't treat them, the infection will catch up with them, and you can treat them then, but maybe they'll never be able to breed back again, so you'll have to beef them in a year. That costs."

On went the rubber glove, up went the arm, and while we all chatted, the arm worked and more and more of the membrane came out. "You know old Charlie, helps out over the gas station?" says the old farmer. "Well, he's not one for making long conversations. Yesterday my boy tried to get him to talk. Tried every which sort of question. He'd say yup, and he'd say nope, but if he couldn't say one or the other, he just sat there and smiled."

Then the old fellow talked about a trip he had just taken to Bridgeport, Connecticut, to see his sister. "Cost me fifteen dollars to stay in a motel."

"Doesn't she have room?"

"No, just a small apartment."

Finally the afterbirth plopped down into the gutter behind the cow. "It's attached with sort of tabs, and you have to get your fingers in there and peel it apart just right so you don't tear the uterine wall. Sometimes a tab or two will want to stay behind, and you've got to find them or they make a mess afterwards."

We left, heading for lunch at the little businessman's restaurant in town nearby. It's hello to a banker, two lawyers, and the head of the town road crew who were eating together in the next booth. A quick bite, a cup of tea, and back to work for the doc.

Doc Mead is atypical in that he hasn't taken the quick route to wealth which lures most young vets—small-animal practice. In the time we made three calls, a small-animal doctor might handle a dozen cats and dogs, and a lizard or two as well. Besides the increased volume, each patient may be asked for a higher fee. The trade magazines reflect business consciousness far more than human medical journals do. There are articles on diseases, but also an article on how to save by building your own pet crematorium, and another article called "Blueprint for Success in the 70's" about how to structure a group practice for maximum volume and profit. I calculated that Doc Mead was making less than half of what he might if he handled more than an occasional small animal. "I don't like the people," he said. "I like farm people."

Man & Tractor

F I HAD KNOWN three years ago what I know now, I never would have bought it. But I learned what I know now because I bought it. Therefore, I should have bought it six years ago, so I would have learned what I know now soon enough to have avoided buying it three years ago—although I would have already owned it then, anyway. . . .

The point may be that there's a silver lining to every cloud. In this case, the cloud is a nineteen-year-old Massey-Harris Pony tractor, a paltry and temperamental little workhorse with the disposition of a prima ballerina and the performance of a dancing bear on an off day.

The silver lining is only discernible after long reference to Norman Vincent Peale. Thank God I had to pay two hundred bucks for replacement parts and machine shop work and thank God I had to spend two weeks in the top of my friend Jim's barn while we rebuilt the engine and thank God the clutch started slipping soon after and needed replacement and thank God the carburetor resists the most sophisticated attempts to adjust it properly. Thank God for all that, because I am learning a bit about fixing a tractor.

Partially because of the tractor, I've met the world of machines and the people who spend their thought and time taming them. But greater revelations lie in the opposite direction; revelations that can only be realized by considering, say, nothing but a certain collar of metal that surrounds the power shaft just aft of the clutch and which, in its better days, served up the throw-out bearing to the stiff but yielding fingers of the pressure plate.

That wee collar has been my partner in a stubby corner of bliss which I am always reluctant to enter because it is not reached without pain, but which is an exquisite joy once gained. Such feelings derive from the, let's call it pleasant reduction of the real world to the clear and bounded study of one demon part. The ecstasy grows as the work proceeds, and is greatest when one is on the verge of unveiling the exact nature of its flaw.

Once the diagnosis is in, there is further joy in the invention-of-ways-around-problems. Does the flexible shaft for the electric drill have a chuck that will take the

cone-shaped wheel? No, but I can replace the wheel's shaft with a narrower bolt. And so on until everything's back together, and I'm making hay again.

Like fishing, politics, and cooking, mechanical work occupies the brain fully and clearly, its presence excluding, at least for brief periods, the dangerous multiplicity that usually keeps us in dread and blandness. The epiphany of sudden mechanical insight is like the moment when the fish strikes, the revolution rumbles with correct and engrossing action, the omelette flips cleanly and shows no signs of browning.

When I bought the tractor, I thought a tractor was a tractor. This one was smaller than most, but still looked quite official. In my greenness, I paid a quarter again what it was worth, shelling out $600 to old Farmer Gurney across the road. He had used it every day for fifteen years, plowing four acres for corn or good mowing, hauling two cans of milk on it to his son-in-law's farm up the next hill because the milk truck would not even try our hill. He ran a saw rig with it each fall, cutting into stove-length at least fifteen cords of slabwood. He hayed seven or eight acres, cutting grass, raking, and hauling a wagon between the barn (now collapsed and rotting and his widow would never part with a board or beam of the wreck) and field, while his son-in-law baled. Then he had a heart attack. The son-in-law bought his cows and parked the tractor in the horse barn. Then I came along and paid too much for it.

At first it ran OK. I got into a deal for a while with my neighbor Bruce, sharing my tractor and his truck.

He was raising beef calves, a commercial sideline which is gaining popularity around here because it supposedly involves little labor once fencing and housing are established. We built the first haystack in Clabberville in thirty years, because there was no baler at hand. Old-timers would drop by and shout up to us, "Comb the sides down more sheer or she won't shed rain like she should." Or, "Don't make no damn wading pool in the middle." He put fences around the stack that the calves could just reach over, and they ate out of the pile all winter. The only work he had to do was to move the fence in every few days, and put bedding (sawdust or straw) on the ground around the stack when it got too messy.

Eventually the tractor broke and we panicked. Neither of us knew anything about motors then. I took it over to Burlingame John, Inc., Tractor Repairs, and they unclogged the radiator, put in new gaskets, and, after bolting the whole thing together again, told me it needed new rings (thin bands around each piston that provide the tight, flexible metal seal necessary for good compression). If they had told me while the thing was still apart, it would have been only an hour's more work to provide them. I suppose they figured that, like most of their other customers, we knew all about our machine and weren't interested in rings. The bill was $60 and it still didn't work well. During the following season, Bruce found a custom farm worker to mow for him, and our deal ended.

After we finished the haystack, I took the tractor back home and went to work skidding out logs from the woods. The tractor died, and I rolled it into the barn and forgot about it, feeling bad and not knowing much about what to do.

Jim came by and said he'd show me. So we winched the little dear onto a truck, took it to Wendell and went to work. The deeper we cut, the more seemed wrong, so we did everything. When we got to the camshaft, I had a sudden vision of unity, for it is truly the brain of the motor, coordinating fuel, electrical, and exhaust systems with inevitable perfection.

The camshaft is not like, for example, the engine block, which is, in its lunkish way, merely the container of what happens. The camshaft is full of intention; it is planned to admit fuel, then cause circuits to trip on and off, then release exhaust, and to do all this for four separate cylinders working in sequence. If you ever are obliged to tear down an engine, regard well the camshaft. It's worth the price of admission.

When it was back together, it ran sweetly and sounded clean and pure. I'd lost my fear of it, because I had understood what most everything was and was learning how to think about its ailments. I plowed a big fall garden and a patch of rutabagas near the woods for the deer to eat, harrowed them both smooth. Later, I mowed ten more acres of hay.

Then the clutch started slipping and chattering. Hank allowed that I might work on it in his shed, because he had tools I might need and might advise me if I got in a jam. It took me two days to split the tractor in half, pull the front and back apart, replace the throw-out bearing and clutch, consider the scored line in the collar, and heal the wound. Then it worked well. I drove home smiling.

Two weeks later, it wouldn't go into gear. Pushing down the clutch pedal had no effect at all. I split the tractor for the second time and discovered that the new, brand spanking new, pressure plate sold me by Massey Ferguson, Inc., was defective (one finger's pivot pin had dropped out). In some way I was happy to learn I hadn't done anything wrong the first time. But there was no particular joy in repeating the labor of two weeks earlier. My time was down from two days to one afternoon, though, and it was interesting because I did the work in Jimmy Barlow's service station and there were plenty of folks coming by to chat.

I once got offered, free, a lovely 1942 Ford farm truck that has run for years on flat tires, with sheet metal hood to replace the rusted original, and no second gear. ("You don't really need it, you know. First and third ain't working too poorly.") I turned it down though. I figure I'd soon spend more time working on it than with it, and I'm content to take my spiritual lessons where I find them.

The Language
of Machines

I AM BY NATURE not much of a leaper into things
—although there are a few exceptions. But I
have learned by now that most chores fixing
machines are, somehow or another, jobs I can
do myself. I grew up in suburbia
and never even suspected
that there was any alternative to
taking broken bikes to Western
Auto, and later, broken cars
to the Bridge Garage.

However, I was not a com-
plete ten-thumbs. I built my
share of birdhouses and, with Dad, an iceboat once,
and I took pride in such homey mechanical victories as
fixing my own typewriter.

I don't see why plumbing and auto mechanics aren't
taught to everyone in high school. The maintenance and
repair of machines has been lifted from the hands of ev-
eryman and left in the hands of a few enlightened trades-

148

men. And like most people placed in the jaws of temptation, most repairmen from garage mechanics to toaster fixers have become an unscrupulous lot best left to their own schemes.

Out here, an older sort of relationship between servicemen and customers is still discernible. Until a few years ago, a carpenter rarely did private work—every farmer could build some sort of house if he had to, and most did at least build barns at one time or another. A carpenter worked full-time in the mill keeping the plant in order. As the shop wore out, one piece at a time, he would be the one to build a new chute or workbench. But household repairs were usually done by the homeowner. If the homeowner was old or infirm, his son or nephew did it, or it didn't get done. In the market towns, a few lawyers and merchants used carpenters as they are used nowadays, but that was exceptional.

It's still true in Clabberville that much of the work done by auto mechanics is done for people who lack the time, inclination, or special tools to do their own work—not for people who lack the understanding to do it. I've sat in the Volvo place down near Amherst College and watched the mechanics patronize returning customers who seemed resigned to being mystified and satisfied by whatever was told to them. And I've sat in Stubb's Garage here, listening to detailed discussions between the repairman and the customers in which the repairman assumed he would be not merely understood but required to account for himself.

Required for any developing mechanical consciousness is attentiveness to the strange and marvelously precise language of the world of machines. I like the clear, cold images conjured up by names of machine parts such as "keyway" or "spline" or of tools such as "driftpin" or "glazebreaker." I am more pleased now to know just

149

what a "bushing" is than I ever was to learn how to say "car" in French or "chariot" in Latin.

I figure that I'm now on a par in mechanical skills with the average thirteen-year-old boy in Clabberville. I have no hope to ever catch up to the eighteen-year-olds. With this growing understanding of the language and process of doing mechanical work has come a telling discovery.

One Saturday afternoon, Rex, whose job involves quality-testing of hard metals at the tap-and-die factory down in the county seat, had us over for a barbecue. After a "fine feed," as it was generally acclaimed to be, the usual town ritual took place: the ladies disappeared with the paper plates and paper tablecloth and the men settled into some "man talk." I felt a little uncomfortable in this company at first and would have preferred to be in on the pickle-making discussion in the kitchen. These men seemed so at ease in dealing with the mysteries of their cars or bantering about the foibles of huge mill machines that I had never even seen.

They were trading stories about car engines. Their stories presented difficult mechanical symptoms and the listeners would try to jump the gun on the storyteller and diagnose the malady even before all the symptoms were on the table. Problems were described and then, I realized, ingenious solutions to the problems were described: "All I had around was a freeze plug from an old Ford Six, but goddamn if I didn't make it fit with a little tampering. Save me twenty bucks, at least." Their solutions were the sort of improvised ones that come with a sudden "aha" and a vision of some odd-looking scrap of metal thrown into the barn years earlier for just such an occasion.

Rex's brother said, "I'm stumped by this one." And he described a particular rattle in his tractor gearbox which only occurred under certain conditions. He didn't know just what it was, and couldn't tell whether he should stop everything to fix it, or whether he could live with it awhile. Various possibilities were argued, tests to prove them devised, and the auto mechanic offered to come take a listen on the way home from work.

It's no accident that these guys, who would be floored if they were ever called "creative" or if they were ever accused of "problem sharing," had held, as they do every day, a discussion whose form would have done any brainstorming meeting of engineers proud.

The most knowledgeable guys were indeed showing virtuoso creativity; the others were shamelessly sharing the knowledge.

It's not very different from the conversations that take place across the supper table on the farms of communal families around here, except that women share in the discussions there. When there are jobs that need doing— when the tractor must be fixed before it can be used to haul the winter wood and the outside water hose must be fitted with a T-joint so it can be drained between uses in winter to avoid freezing—it seems plausible to learn to do those jobs.

For me, tending machines turns out to be not very far removed from tending a garden, at least in the sense that they both put some reality back into the basic acts of living. In fact, it was gardening that led me to mechanics. I bought that twenty-year-old tractor "that works real good—never used much," plowed half a potato patch with it, learned what the funny sound was that it made just before it died, fixed it, and ate potatoes come fall. The potatoes taught me about the carburetor. The tomatoes soon taught me about the brakes. So maybe things are sort of related, if you squint your eyes and look at them the right way.

Summer Solstice

SUMMER SOLSTICE, my third away from town, and my first decadent party. I spent years as a student and no decadent parties. I hung around with hippies late and soon, and no decadent parties.

But here on the mountain, in the midst of bright sun and long hours haying, a decadent party. It started clean, over at Yago's, a quiet midsummer celebration; talk among old friends who had shared the day's work and tested each other's tempers. We cooked together, decked the table with the fruits of our labor, and sat out of doors amidst the blood and down of the goose we slaughtered, smiling and eating, bantering in a way which hid neither love for nor impatience with each other. It was a comfortable meal.

The boys in the band gathered, the music was struck loud, we danced and dashed madly around, hugged each other and wept, silly with wine. And that was all OK. It seemed natural enough.

Then I found myself, as if cast out of Eden, among the same friends, but the party had moved (I must have dozed on the way) to the fancy new digs of Arthur Aardvark. He'd built it himself. It is a fit site for one of those parties they have pictures of in *Playboy*. Arthur had built himself a loft living room high enough to offer a second balcony to look down upon a first balcony, a first balcony from which a few pensive party-goers considered the geometry of the gathering below.

And I noticed that many of the revelers were naked. Not that anyone had been particularly dressed earlier in the night, but that it suddenly mattered. Arthur had bustled in with a ladder and had slung a plank swing from the ridgepole. Now a pudgy fellow, his sex almost hidden in the folds of thighs and paunch, was giggling and pushing Arthur in the swing. Arthur, sporting pegged gabardine plaid slacks and a white turtleneck, pumped gracefully, soaring about his own new house. Perhaps Arthur had rigged the swing before, perhaps first measuring off the rope and tying in the plank while still building the house. Had he clambered onto it sweaty in his carpenters' whites and had he pumped gracefully on that virgin ride aloft over stacks of lumber and half-used cans of paint?

You know who was naked at Arthur's party? It wasn't the commune couples who take off their clothes when they get hot working in the garden. It wasn't Arthur, who, as described, was dressed properly for the occasion. It was the boys and girls come up for the occasion from U. Mass. and Smith, and who were having themselves a whale of a good time.

I left a bit sad, taking the back roads twenty miles

from the farm, a bit high, disoriented and lost on the unfamiliar route, but too listless to be impatient. Finally I came to the road I recognized, and found myself out of the woods and nearer home than I'd expected.

The next day the shock of dawn woke me. The sun shone more fiercely than it had in a week and because the sunrise gleamed so yellow, the new daffodils under the window appeared white. The barn swallows wriggled as they chattered on the high-tension wires outside, and their sound seemed to come from inside my ears.

I couldn't sleep for the noise. Filled with that sort of exciting animated exhaustion which one feels after a hard day and three hours of sleep, I brewed some coffee. Before six, I found myself in the woods, following the old Blanding's Brook Road down the hill. Where it passes over high ledges, one can see the marks of stone chisels on the fresh-cracked rock faces, sheared off when the road was built. They used to drill a line of holes down into a rock they wished to move, wait until fall, and fill the holes with water. After a freeze a crack might connect the holes. More water, another freeze, and the rock finally worked loose enough to pry up. The slab ripped from the ledge above the brook can still be seen, half swallowed by an old maple that must have stopped its tumble down the hill a hundred years ago when the road was built.

I followed the road, treading on trillium, columbine, and on the stinking daisies which had taken over the cleared patch just above Floyd's place.

Perhaps this sounds a bit self-conscious; I am trying not to be bashful about my own earnestness, and these are serious things I want to tell you. For just past the clearing with the daisies, behind a log, I found a beautiful white deer skull, picked clean by scavengers and undis-

154

turbed since the picking. I carried it off in the crook of
my arm, much as Hamlet, of course, might carry poor
Yorick's skull.

I hadn't gone far before I heard the solid thunk of ax
hitting tree, and not much farther yet before I came
upon old Floyd himself, doing a bit of work while his
wife cooked breakfast. Floyd spent thirty-nine years
pulling a cart full of metal parts about the mill down in
the Basin, and no discussion of him fails to mention his
remarkable strength. "I've seen him unload a truckload
of two-hundred-pound sacks, one on each shoulder, all
day and not tire a bit," someone once said.

I've seen him hobble up the hill (for now he is lame with arthritis and last year had a scrape with death that had him a month in the hospital) and when he got to the top, lift the front end of my car out of a snowbank.

We chatted for a few minutes about what we'd planted new in our gardens, and about how hot the days were getting, and about whether I might have better luck with my pigs this year than I did last. I asked him how he was feeling (all the while holding the deer skull, which neither of us mentioned), and he told me in some detail about where it hurt. This made me think that he must hurt quite a bit. He'd always before said he felt great, even when he couldn't possibly have felt very well at all.

Finally, he took the skull from my hands, rolled it over in his palms, and said, "It's been the hardest winter I ever remember for quite a few years. Barns come down that stood as long as I knew about them. And lots of these deer here"—he shook the skull a bit—"must have found the going too tough this year. It wasn't so much the snow, though that drifted clear up to the eaves in the back of the house. I think the wind is getting stronger. Took more wood to keep the house warm than I ever remember. Wind sucks the heat right out."

Then he smiled, handed back the skull. "You won't believe this," he said, "but I'm gonna tell you anyway. There was one day about February the wind blew so strong it took two other men just to hold my hat on my head!" We both laughed loud and deep and his face turned red, and then he took his ax and went back to work, and I took my deer skull and padded back up the hill to see who might be awake.

Hay

I NEVER USED TO NOTICE how much the weather varies within ten or fifteen miles. "Down to" the county seat (once a market town for all the farms of the county and now a gathering of shopping centers) they have already been cutting hay for three weeks when we are just getting started. One farmer I noticed there takes a first cutting of rye grass from his cornfield at the end of May and then plows in the stubble and plants feed corn. Two crops from one field! Unheard of out here in the mountains. We thought that only happened in Georgia.

Hay cutting starts here about the tenth of June, and hay cut before the first of July has "the most goodness." As it matures past a certain point, the digestible protein content drops markedly, and the grass becomes woody and less palatable, so cows want to eat less of it. There is another pressure toward early mowing. If the grass gets too high, much of it will topple over or "lodge"—a condition that makes it difficult to mow. In February you can find advertisements in the newspaper, "Good Hay for Sale: 50¢ a bale. June cut: 75¢," and the more expensive hay is the first to go.

Hay is the principal bulk fed to dairy cows, and a fresh (recently calved) mother might eat twenty-five pounds of it a day. If hay is replaced by the same quantity of "better" feed, with less crude fiber content,

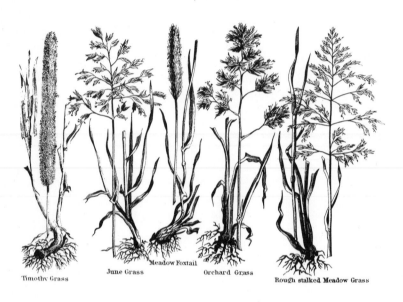

Timothy Grass   June Grass   Meadow Foxtail   Orchard Grass   Rough stalked Meadow Grass

cream production may plunge drastically. It takes a lot of good hay to keep thirty or forty cows healthy. And it takes a lot of room to store it. Traditionally, the hayloft is above the cows, where the hay insulates their quarters during the winter and may easily be dropped to the animals.

Making good hay is a craft that may be perfected only through years of experience. To start with, it is hard to keep a mowing in the rich legumes and broad-leafed

158

grasses which cure to the best hay, in fescue and timothy, bromegrass and bird's-foot trefoil, red clover, vetch, alfalfa, and Sudan grass. A hayfield in this area undergoes a four- or five-year cycle of degeneration, starting from the time it is seeded. Year by year, the proportion of "native" to seeded grasses will increase. The native grasses, while not as heavily leafed nor bred for high protein content or palatability to cattle, will by all

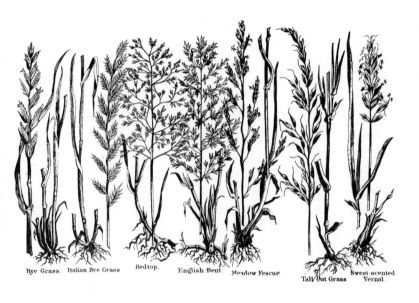

Rye Grass   Italian Rye Grass   Redtop   English Bent   Meadow Fescue   Tall Oat Grass   Sweet-scented Vernal

odds be more aggressive than the seeded grasses. They will spread tough roots to steal their food, grow in packed clusters to crowd out the new pudgy cousins whose ancestors were brought up in feather-soft beds at agricultural colleges and seed company farms.

Corn and hay are frequently alternated in three-year cycles. Corn depletes the soil. Usually chemical fertilizers and manure are spread to meet the heavy demands of the corn. Fertilizer has a cumulative effect as it breaks down in the soil. In order to "get full mileage out of his fertilizer dollar" a farmer usually feels he must plant corn until the soil will no longer make the work of growing it profitable. Then the corn is followed with a seeding of legume-rich grass seed. The legume family (including vetch, alfalfa, ladino, beans, and peas) fixes nitrogen as it grows, replenishing the soil and helping to support grasses grown with it. Some of the legumes are very fussy and won't take well in soil which is too wet, dry, sandy, clayey, or, especially, too sour or acid. So things must be made just right.

I look at the dry, yellow, odorless soil of a typical third-year cornfield and I am appalled. The farmers around here, with one or two exceptions, are not kind to their land. They burn it with huge doses of chemicals. It would be kinder to the lively organic community dwelling in the dirt were the chemicals applied in several small doses, but labor costs make that difficult. They plow the ground with moldboard plows to the same depth each year, sometimes creating by their repeated packing of the earth a "hardpan" or "plowsole"—an impermeable layer of earth that interferes with both drainage after storms and capillary action to keep topsoil moist during droughts. They dump Atrazine-type weedkiller onto the cornfields, stuff that is designed to defoliate everything not named corn. And they spray with nasty pesticides which must exterminate as many friends as enemies of the farmer, and also make him one of the chief supporters of the thriving chemical industry.

The soil, left to its own ineluctable ways, tends and heals itself. The community which lives among the roots of plants includes everything from moles (no good) through earthworms (very good) down to microorganisms (good ones eat bad ones for supper). Disturb this balance, and you take on the obligation of contending with whatever monsters survive man's tampering.

So it is that a corn blight left recent corn crops frequently off-taste and sparse, not just in western Massachusetts (where the effects were relatively slight) but all over the country. And so it is that nationwide blights, specific to particular cash crops, require constant development of new resistant breeds and new poisons which can keep ahead of the mutating infections.

Nevertheless, I would be at fault if you were left with a distorted sense of imminent disaster from hearing one man say his piece. The disaster is slow (it too is obeying the rules of nature) and does not mean bankruptcy to every farmer who practices standard methods of farming. It does mean that he is subjected to a binding economic relationship with manufacturers of fertilizers, pesticides, and special equipment, and that he leaves the ground a little worse off than he finds it.

But (to take up where I left off a few paragraphs back) when Farmer Jones seeds down his depleted and much abused cornland with grasses and clovers, the grasses and clovers will indeed come up, and the field will bear lush green grass.

What happens next? If he is lucky, Jones has found a day since finishing his corn planting to put in a family vegetable garden. He will need another day to jockey all the haying equipment (mower, conditioner, side delivery rake, tedder, baler, hay wagon) out of storage, replace the broken parts he forgot to fix during the winter, and grease and oil the hundreds of obscure joints and portals that want grease and oil.

Unless a field is badly lodged, mowing and conditioning go on at the same time. The mower is a long sickle bar that hangs underneath the tractor and extends off to the right. Farmer Jones (or his son) will ride around and around the field (clockwise, from the outside, so as not to ride over the uncut hay). The conditioner, dragged behind the tractor, scoops up the cut hay and cracks and crushes the stems between rollers. This cuts at least a day off the required drying time and also makes the hay more digestible.

Ah, the glory in finishing the last swath in a large field. It is usually late in the afternoon. The stings suffered earlier in the day from mowing up a wasps' nest have stopped smarting. Evening breezes cool the fevered brow, and one might even shut off the tractor for a moment and, in the ringing quiet which follows a day of riding in the roar of the diesel engine, consider the few missed patches and sniff the fragrance of the fresh cutting.

Last year, perched as described, I was treated to an amazing sight. All the barn swallows had come together from all the barns in the town for an easy meal of bugs shaken out of the fallen grass. I had all but ceased to notice them when their cry grew suddenly alarmed. A hawk had dived into their midst and was pursuing one small bird. Agile as she was, she did not seem to possess the strength to get away. But instead of fleeing, the rest of the swallows turned on the hawk. They pecked at his eyes and belly, driving him repeatedly from the attack. I lost the fray as it careened over the top of a hill past the end of the field.

As the late June evening falls, Farmer Jones may be seen tedding into the sunset. What's a tedder? A machine whose spring steel prongs stir up the hay, toss it into the air, and allow it to fall lightly down again, where it may dry more easily and shake off the night dew more quickly the next day. Farmers in some regions never ted.

The next day the hay will be gathered by a side deliver rake into windrows. The fallen blades will be fluffed and rolled into a long thin row, perhaps two feet high, and as continuous as possible, spiraling toward the center of the field. This allows the hay to dry readily in the wind and sultry air, while protecting much of it from the searing sun. The following day, or perhaps late the same day, the rake may be used to rotate the windrow one hundred and eighty degrees so the bottom may dry as well.

The second or third day after cutting (rain, of course, throws the whole operation off), baling begins. A fancy hay baler, costing more than a new car and used fifteen days each summer, is nevertheless a masterpiece of technology. It scoops up the windrows of hay, compresses them into rectangular bales weighing thirty to sixty pounds, and then binds them with baling twine, tying neat knots as it finishes its work.

The bales fall off the end of the baler, whence they are picked up by hand, stacked on wagon and truck, transported to haymow or loft, and there restacked in a manner planned to allow winter access to the right piles at the right times. This job is the hardest work of the whole haying process, and in fact is nearly the hardest work on the farm all year. I have seen muscle-bound city jocks toss around the bales for an hour and stagger off the field in near exhaustion, while Farmer Jones' beanpole son lopes along, tossing bales from noon till sunset. It gives me satisfaction to see such a debacle, and I believe it gives Jones more satisfaction yet.

In the old days, before the advent of sickle bars and balers, hay was scythed by hand, turned by hand, raked by hand, and gathered loose into carts. Even after horse or tractor sickling was common and hayrakes eliminated that manual labor, hay was still gathered loose and stored in mows deep enough to allow it to compress almost to bale tightness. At feeding time, a chunk would be sawed out of mow or stack with a relic called the hay knife. Taking in loose hay isn't much harder than taking in baled hay, but at the end of a day, only about a third as much will have moved from field to barn.

Nowadays, on the large farms which can afford the huge capital outlays for elegant equipment, things have gone the other way in the past few years. A machine called a windrower mower will cut, condition, and curl into a windrow a gigantic swath of hay in a single pass. When the hay is dried, another machine will bale it, toss the bales back to mechanical arms which stack them tight, and then will off-load the wagon of bales automatically in place in a storage shed. If this keeps up, farmers of the future will have the pear-shaped figures of today's bus drivers.

Captain Cat
of Clabberville

As any writer soon realizes, the best information comes from marginal people—those half in the world of whatever-is-happening, and half in the world of those who are curious about it. If I can tell you about life in the country, it is because of (not, as may sometimes appear, in spite of) my time spent as a full-fledged member of the world of students, politics, scenes, and such other hoop-dee-do as fills lives back there.

There's a sort of Captain Cat of Clabberville, a fellow who has run the gas station at Clabberville three corners since the early 1920's, who has grown to be in his own way very much on the margin of the local world and at the same time a dependable source of knowledge about it. He's not especially keen on local scuttlebutt, although I'm sure Clabbervillians could be illuminated by his knowledge of the quirks of the grandparents of whomever is being whispered about today. He prefers to talk about old machines, old institutions, old families—including his own—and old memories.

His name is Jimmy Barlow, and he is old himself—born in 1895 and quick to tell you so. Yet his vigor is startling and would be if he were only fifty. Jimmy gets up soon after dawn and can be seen in the first light jogging to the post office and home again. He might then pick up his chain saw and work trimming a nearby woodlot he owns, and still be open for the first customers on their way to the county seat for the day shift.

As he works, his motions have the sharp articulation you see now and then in someone who seems to derive satisfaction from the sheer act of moving. So it is when Jimmy pumps gas, checks oil or air, washes windshields for men a quarter his age. He is always cordial and willing to hear about most anything anyone wants to say.

Jimmy is a great listener and takes such pleasure in

hearing new tales that one may altogether forget he's doing far more listening than talking.

The habit has won him a mongrel and diverse erudition which he is not quick to display, and which might well surprise some of his oldest customers. He's a smart one, and was always experimenting with some new tool. He reads the *Christian Science Monitor* daily and is eager to discuss its eclectic features with his friends. Photographs he took as long ago as 1913 show style not yet dated.

Three or four of his photos are tacked up next to the garage's cash register—one shows his fellow Marines dapper in spanking and creased uniforms just before the Marne; another portrays his brothers and sisters arranged in a straggling line, the youngest still in knickers. They are standing on a hill. Far below can be seen the Clabberville papermill where several of them subsequently worked thirty or forty years, and which still provides one ancient sister with a monthly pension check.

Still another is a self-portrait, a three-quarters view taken in the light of a window. There's Jimmy, natty and alert at twenty-five, sporting a rakish fedora and staring intently out the window. His hand is caught squeezing the rubber bulb, just as it ignited the flash powder and tripped the shutter so long ago.

The large photographs were not Jimmy's idea. He had had the negatives around for years, and one day got to chatting with some fellow who passed through frequently. The fellow turned out to be a photographer teaching in the area. Jimmy has not the usual tradesman's sharp eye for outsiders. He sees the new wave of city expatriates not so much as well-heeled customers but as well-informed conversationalists. Newcomers quickly discover his interest, as I did not so many years ago, and seek his advice on matters ranging from the digging of outhouses to whose boy might mow lawns.

Only once have I seen Jimmy abandon his usual attitude —one that might be termed "cordial reticence"—and throw modesty to the winds. I had stopped down with this friend of mine, whose misfortune it is to come from a grand blueblood Yankee family whose name is "known." "Jimmy Barlow," I said, "this is Oakes Plimpton."

"Plimpton?" says Jimmy. "That's quite an old family. You know, I'm related to Cotton Mather." He went on to provide an avalanche of detail about the bloodline—a very elegant pedigree too. Oakes and he compared notes at length, even finding some distant grand-aunt in common. I stood on the sidelines, silently invoking the memory of minions of Polish rabbis, Russian horsetraders, Lithuanian schoolmasters, all nameless.

Not only has Jimmy a fancy family, but he may well be the richest man in Clabberville. "How did you get so much land—you never farmed?" I asked him once.

"I bought it when it was cheap!" he answered. "And I didn't sell much of it."

He's asked frequently nowadays if he will think of "parting with" this piece of woodlot or that chunk of pastureland, but he almost always declines. He has a professional's knowledge of timbering and makes some of his income by contracting selective cutting of his land. He spends spare Sundays at work on it, improving access roads and trimming deadwood from young pines so they will grow knot-free wood for the length of one or two sawlogs. Wood lot management is a gift of industriousness for future generations. Jimmy's work pruning last weekend may be worth $50 to someone thirty years from now.

Jimmy must feel ageless. Pruning is not the only activity of his in which he shows determination to become a centenarian. As I was fixing my tractor over there once, I overheard an old-car freak chatting up Jimmy.

"I hear you have a Caddy twelve cylinder block. I might be able to use one if the price is right," says the car freak.

Jimmy knows who he is, so he's got the winning play; the car freak thinks he might possibly be passing for the boy next door, just looking for some spare parts to keep his jalopy running. If he'd come clean, I figure Jimmy would have given him the thing—I've seen him more generous than that. But his manner seemed all bluster. Jimmy responded in kind.

"I suppose it ought to be worth quite a bit. I've kept it over thirty years." At this point the car freak's smile faded. Jimmy went on, "And if you don't think so, I'll keep it another thirty years until it is." Jimmy paid no mind to the fact that at the time of the proposed later transaction, he would be 106. The car freak might have felt intimidated by the realization, and quickly settled up for twenty bucks.

Jimmy's seeming agelessness grew out of a scrape with death he had nine years ago. The county hospital had looked him over, told him they couldn't find any trouble, and sent him home. In something that could only be an act of love on the part of an old friend, the local doctor stubbornly persisted in his own concern, pored over the X-rays one night, and discovered a small cancer. "His extra effort saved my life. That's sure," Jimmy says. Now the doc has suffered a stroke and only sees patients once in a while, and then only if he's known them for years. Many afternoons he can be found down at Jimmy's sitting in front of the candy display, shooting the breeze with two or three of the older fellows who congregate there. It's a different class of old-timers than the gang that frequents the Clabberville Inn, and certainly is nothing like the crowd down at the Rotary.

I can't help thinking they are the local wise men, although that could only be my own youthful foolishness. They discuss the weather and get it right; they discuss the war, bussing, welfare, all with a kindness which is the more surprising because of its context.

"You ought to have a potbellied stove in the middle of the garage, so everyone can sit around and spit on it," I suggested once.

"I did," Jimmy said, "but the insurance made me get rid of it."

As they sit, they keep an eye on Jimmy, who only joins their talk between gas customers and tire changes. I caught his older brother marveling and shaking his head once while he watched Jimmy swatting a tire rim with a four-pound hammer to break the bead on a flat.

The first thing anybody says when they talk about Jimmy is, "He's a lucky fellow." Although they are referring to his scrape with death, he's lucky in more ways still, and in a very traditional sense. He's gotten wealthy by grace of his own wit (although he may suspect that good blood tells), he has a nice wife with whom he still laughs and makes jokes, his kids have "done him proud" —one is a missionary in Central America, another an engineer, a third, a "G-man." And most important, his company is sought because he includes those about him in an aura of sensibleness and calm—his conversation assumes one is decent, industrious, and at least as well informed as himself.

Yet perhaps because of his success, he has transcended Clabbervillian values. His intelligence, friendliness, and curiosity, his business success, the growing contrast between his health and the health of his friends, and especially his illness of nine years ago have given him a sharp sense of the nature of the institutions which made him. He has taken recently to filling the blank pages of old diaries with scrawled recollections of curious adventures and long accounts of things as they used to be.

On the page marked March 2, 1968, he has written, "In 1917, I sat in the chair of A——— D———, dentist, of Clabberville, having several teeth filled. Just over one year later, I was back in a dentist's chair, this time in France, behind the front lines. I remarked to the dentist that I had been in the office of A——— D——— a year before and he told me the two had shared quarters at dental school." The next entry is headed "Things My Mother Used to Store for the Winter" and lists perhaps fifty foodstuffs, from winter squash to six or seven varieties of apples, to hams and mutton. I think he writes these things to keep himself located in the changing world. But he has not stayed still in his own values.

Not long ago he sold a parcel of land to the Vermont Conservancy, including the very beautiful cut of the East Branch, North River, known as "the Gorge." He sold it to them at a fraction of its worth to a developer, on the condition that it remain unexploited and open to whomever knows how to find it.

Reading my own words about Jimmy, I fear they sound a bit eulogistic. He's out there pumping gas and listening to the world, and at the rate he's going he may, in fact, be doing the same thing in thirty years' time.

Wood Heat

MY FIRST ACQUAINTANCE with the chore of gathering wood came from *Little Lulu* Comics. Lulu's bedtime tales to Alvin about Witch Hazel usually started out with a little poor girl who looked surprisingly like Lulu gathering either beebleberries or faggots of wood, depending upon the season.

In the fashion of the most noble tragedies, Lulu was portrayed as a high-born princess, stricken by hard times. Gathering beebleberries and wood was supposed to show just how far she had fallen: all that stood between full Lulu and starvation was her own fast hand at the beebleberry, and all that stood between warm Lulu and Lulu as an ice block was her own labor in the woods.

If our farmhouse had had oil heat, I'd not have thought twice when we first moved in about calling the oilman and firing the thing up. Then it would have been the oilman, the pipeline man, the oilwell men, the geologists, the technicians, and the mogul financiers who rule America all standing between warm Mark and Mark as an ice block.

By good fortune, the house had escaped modernization. The rural electrification campaign of the late forties did entice old Levi to link up, but that was only for light to read the Bible. Water for the house still flows from a spring farther up the hill, and in the winter, heat still pours into a central foyer ("the heat room") and then seeps about the rest of the house from a huge, old, single-stack half-human wood furnace named Atlas.

Atlas sits on a concrete slab in the middle of the basement and, in the manner of his namesake, appears to hold up the house. A single fat cylinder leads heat upstairs and is surrounded by a wider cylinder of sheet metal which leads cool air from upstairs back down for recycling. If you can imagine all the warmth from all the radiators in a four-bedroom house shimmering up from a single heating grate, you will have some idea of Atlas' formidable

powers. Almost all winter we have a full-time sauna/mitten-drying/bread/rising room.

I say almost all winter because we're on the north face of the mountain, and when the wind blows very hard, we feel it.

On January nights when the wind batters past the house it sucks the heat right out with it, and even with all the vents opened wide Atlas can barely keep the pipes from freezing. There's nothing to do then but crawl into the sack, pile on quilts, and try not to be the first one up.

The first one up fills Atlas. At first I used to get up in the middle of the night and reload. If I didn't, there would be no fire at all come morning, a cold house and a cold bit of work, loading, adjusting the air intake and damper, adding larger and larger wood, before the fire leveled off for the day.

Then Floyd Kendrick, the wise old fellow down the road, suggested that for the night fire, why didn't I load the logs so they stood up on end in the firebox. It took some experimenting but once I mastered the fine points, it worked and with the right wood the fire now will burn for as long as twelve hours.

A wood furnace (or any hot-air furnace) has two separate air systems, sealed off from each other. One, for the blaze, draws cold outside air in to supply oxygen to the fire, and then passes smoke through stovepipe into a chimney and on out. The other system collects cool household air from the floor and circulates it over the top of the firebox where it is heated and then rises back upstairs.

Atlas has a variety of controls, all affecting the airflow to and from the blaze: a loading door with sliding air vents, a lower door that can be opened to let drafts of cold air roar up through the firebox, a damper (which is a metal plate inside the stovepipe) that can be turned to close off most of the flow of air through the stovepipe to the chimney, and a check draft which is a hatch in the side of the same stovepipe that, when open, slackens the blaze by allowing air to be drawn into the chimney without ever passing through the firebox at all.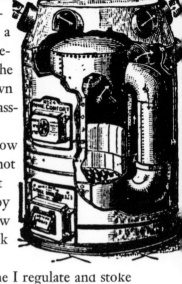

How long the fire lasts and how hot it burns are both affected not only by setting these controls but also by how the wood is placed, by the type of wood used, and by how green it is. In local idiom, dry rock maple "has the most heat in it."

I get great satisfaction every time I regulate and stoke the furnace. It is like a winter-long chess problem, with the impetus of necessity thrown in to make it all real. For example, the six p.m. filling must provide heat for an evening at play downstairs, but must also end up consuming all the wood in the furnace, leaving a bed of hot coals, and plenty of room for loading in the upright night fire. Other times have other requirements, and the moderate intricacy of it all gets to be second nature after a while. Last winter I felt I'd turned into a human thermostat, and then realized that's what I'd been all along.

They say wood heats three times, once for the cutting, once for the stacking, and once for the burning. I wonder why the folk-wit who invented that one left out the carrying, loading on and off the truck, splitting and tossing into the woodshed, and hauling from shed to furnace.

Atlas burns about ten cords of wood a winter—a stack four feet high, four feet wide, and eighty feet long. It takes two of us about a week of hard work to cut it, which may be a bit longer than it takes genuine country folk. This year, it took six of us a long day and two trucks to draw it out of the woods.

I always find cutting to be nasty work. The chain saw is loud and requires frequent tinkering. And parts of the job seem very dangerous. Trees fall in unexpected directions; one tree bounced after hitting the ground and its trunk shot backwards past us. Another tree nearly fell on top of me when I was fool enough to underestimate its height while dragging it down with a rope. Had I been standing six inches right or left I would be dead now.

It has led me to be extremely cautious and I have reverted to a "when my number's up" fatalism. The caution has paid off to date.

Corn

WHEN I WAS about fourteen, somebody's ma drove us to the Long Trail in upper Connecticut and left us for a two-day hike. We walked a bit and ate sandwiches, trudged a good piece more, ate some more sandwiches, some oranges, some cake, and some more sandwiches, walked on a bit, and decided to stop for supper. Finding precious little left in the larder, we doubled back in the last of the daylight to a cornfield we'd just passed, harvested eight or ten ears, and stumbling on roots and rocks in the dark made it to our evening camp. Sluggo boiled the water, Henry threw in the corn, and—it tasted awful. It was like biting right through the carton into a box of cornstarch.

If we were cows we would have loved it, because it was—I know now—what is called field corn, feed corn, or just plain "corn," the last name assuming that the stuff for humans is called "sweet corn." Field corn has come a long way since the white man ran off the last Indian who dared till a field of maize around here. It's been selected and crossbred to obtain the qualities farmers want when they grow corn to feed cows.

What do they want? Corn is grown for high yield. With common farming practices, corn will produce more feed, and therefore more gallons of milk per acre than any other crop that a dairyman can choose. Field corn will grow nine or ten feet high (there's no reason for sweet corn to grow high at all—it only increases the likelihood of wind damage). It will have broad leaves (but not so tough or fibrous as to trouble a gourmandizing heifer), a strong stalk, an aggressive and quick-starting taproot system, and will yield at least two good ears of corn as well. It will ripen in a chosen number of days (usually about 110 in western Massachusetts) to the proper stage for harvesting. The ear will be long, its kernels full and deep.

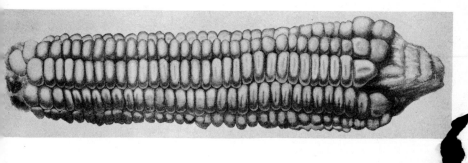

Usually corn is planted as soon as possible after the danger of frost has passed. Wonderful old Solon Robinson, who wrote an agricultural newspaper column just before the Civil War, passes along what he assures us is a genuine "old Indian rule": "When in the spring should corn be planted? When the leaves upon the oak trees are as large as the ears of the squirrels that sun themselves on the branches."

One of the advantages of corn over hay as a source of roughage is that a field, once sown, needs little attention until the very end of summer. During the first month before the corn shades competing plants, weeds are a big problem. Many farmers today use some form of herbicide, such as Atrazine, which kills most weeds almost as soon as they come up. It is, I am told, an amazing feat of modern agricultural science. The chemical intrudes itself in the protein synthesis chain of most weed plants, but not the slightly different protein synthesis chain of corn, which goes on growing as if nothing odd was happening.

Many farmers like it because it saves them several days of labor previously spent on a tractor, dragging a cultivator between the corn rows to hoe up weeds. In this case I dare, for all my inexperience, to differ with those who, as a matter of course, spray herbicides on their fields.

When I came for the first time to my farm a few years ago, there were two corn patches, one high up the hill and one below the barn, each of about two sloping acres, filled with the mangiest and poorest field corn ever to cast its shadow on the rich soil of Clabberville. The land had been rented for the previous eight seasons to five taciturn brothers named Glump, who are described by kindest of Clabbervillians as "old-fashioned-type and as "always late—cutting hay once a summer and getting their corn in at least before the Fourth of July." "Old-fashioned" describes practices similar to those which have devastated so much of America's lately rich virgin soil.

Each year the Glumps lavished corn patches with herbicide, using the logic that "if a little does some good, then a lot will work still better." They felt the same way about strong fertilizers which, applied regularly and copiously, will harden and dry the soil by killing off its microorganic matter. The Glumps grew this corn on the "flowerpot" theory, envisioning the ground as that which keeps plants from plummeting downward clear to China, and as a convenient holder of man-made plant food.

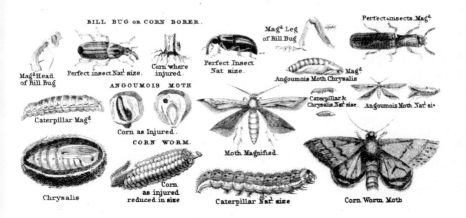

BILL BUG or CORN BORER.

Mag.ᵈ Head of Bill Bug

Perfect insect Nat. size.

Corn where injured.

Perfect Insect Nat size.

Mag.ᵈ Leg of Bill Bug

Perfect insects Mag.ᵈ

Angoumois Moth Chrysalis

Mag.ᵈ

ANGOUMOIS MOTH

Caterpillar Mag.ᵈ

Corn as Injured.

CORN WORM.

Moth Magnified.

Caterpillar & Chrysalis Nat. size.

Angoumois Moth Nat. si•

Chrysalis

Corn as injured reduced in size

Caterpillar Nat. size

Corn Worm Moth

However generous they were with herbicide and strong fertilizer the Glumps did not feel so inclined to spread ground limestone, as they do on fields they own instead of rent. So the pH of the soil declined from a healthy 6.8 to a sour, forboding 4.9, fit stuff for acid-loving sourgrass, small wild strawberries, and creeping patches of moss.

When I came on the scene a *tabula rasa*, free of any contaminating opinions at all about agriculture, I was curious nevertheless about why the cornstalks were virtually ear-free and shoulder high in the best spots. The Glumps cut their corn, skedaddled, and certainly never asked about renting the fields another year. I watched as fall rains carried away the topsoil—the little of it that remained after so many years of similar mismanagement—and wondered about the "contour plowing" I'd read about in my high school history books.

The next spring I tried to start seedlings in boxes filled with soil I'd dug from the upper corn patch. A few sprouts struggled up an inch or two, turned brown, and died. I figured gardening must be extremely difficult, started asking questions of my neighbors, and soon understood that I had been planting in a flat filled with poisoned dirt. I tried again with clean soil, and this time it was easy.

However, the damage to the side-hill corn patches remained, and still remains three years and three tons of limestone per acre later. It is common practice to follow a corn crop with a late fall planting of winter rye grass. The amazing stuff will sprout despite dank fog and freezing nights, will quickly lay down a hairlike net of fibrous roots, and will hold soil in place through the harshest winters. In spring when it is plowed into the ground, the green matter, and more important still the dense mat of roots, quickly decay and increase the organic content of the soil. The field becomes a finer home for the next crop and harbors moisture, earthworms, and a host of wee creatures that have for untold millennia been nature's way of controlling plagues, blights, rusts, molds, parasites, and all manner of infestations.

How can you plant a cover crop of rye when the soil is filled with herbicide? The stuff not only is bad for the soil (but good for the chemical industry/Agriculture Department complex), it also prevents other good practices—such as the sowing of winter cover and green manure crops.

At any rate, one way or another, corn grows all summer, troubled these past few years by southern corn blight, helped by ample rainfall and sunny weather. As it ripens, it attracts skunks and raccoons. Farmers, finding the ragged, torn husks which coons leave behind, will

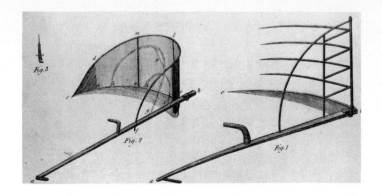

call in the few local sportsmen who keep coon dogs.
They'll come into the cornfields in the dark of night.
Soon the dogs will howl, tree the coon, and the master
of the hunt will appear under the treed coon and plaster
it. Bang. Good for the corn farmers; bad for the coons.
Still other farmers plant a square of sweet corn around
each cornpatch. "The coons get to the sweet corn, and
they think it's so grand they don't see the need to go any
further into the field," explained one old-timer.

When the corn begins to dry up late in the growing
season, a crease develops in the top of each kernel. This
is known as "early dent" and it means the corn is as nutritious as it will ever be, and folks better hustle out and
chop it right away.

For most of the last century, corn was grown strictly
for the ears. The cobs were shucked, dried, and stripped
of their grain. The grain was cracked, ground, and perhaps boiled, and was fed to cows, pigs, and chickens. For
some farming, corn is still a grain crop and is handled
basically the same way. But most dairy farmers now use
the entire above-ground plant—stalk, leaves, and ears.

Starting in the last quarter of the nineteenth century,
a method was made popular for preserving corn to use as
palatable high-energy roughage. The practice of making

ensilage of green plants is relatively new. It was done in Germany for some time before its importation, but didn't become popular until it was tried on a few farms in the southern U.S. and the results publicized.

Silos, which of course are those cylindrical structures standing next to barns, are round for good reason. The first ones were square, and many of them burst because of the tremendous internal pressure they must bear. Also, the corner seams loosened, and the silage inside used to spoil. Silos were frequently made of tongue and groove slats ringed every few feet (more frequently at base than peak) with steel straps. Now they are built of tile, or else of fiber glass and steel as you can see on really fancy, prosperous spreads. Farmers today also make silage in trenches and mounds.

A plain, old, not-too-modern New England dirt farmer harvests corn nowadays by driving through the field with a "single-head corn chopper" in tow behind the tractor. This machine cuts the base of each stalk, then eats the plant, digests it, and expels a heavy rain of small corn shreds from a high-arching pipe down into a dump truck which is chasing along behind the contraption. The dump truck trundles load after load of the chopped corn to the silo, where it is dumped into a silo loader—a trough with a big fat auger lying in the bottom that screws corn chips to one end. There they are blown thirty feet up a stovepipe and into the silo. This chore goes on for a month, whenever the sun shines. An immense quantity must be taken in because a cow will easily consume each day thirty-five or forty pounds of ensilage, as well as a copious amount of good hay and expensive protein supplement. In return, she offers milk—up to eighty pounds (about ten gallons) per day for a quite good and newly freshened cow—and many tens of pounds of manure to return to the cornfield.

Making silage is an art. The size of the chopped pieces must become smaller (down to a quarter inch) as the moisture content of the corn decreases late in the chopping season. Every day farm kids are sent into the silo to run around and wrestle for a while, in order to pack the corn more densely. There is always the danger that deadly "silo gas"—nitrogen dioxide—may develop. In a leaky old wooden silo it dissipates and does no one harm, but every town boasts a few casualties or lifetime cripples to remind the others of the need for caution.

When the silage is packed to exclude all air, a heat-generating process of fermentation begins, which continues for about two weeks. If everything has been done just right, lactic acid-producing bacteria will predominate, and the resulting pickle will tickle the palate of the most fickle cow.

Lactic acid bacteria grow best when the reaction raises the temperature of the silo to eighty or one hundred degrees. If it is too cool, awful-tasting butyric acid silage will form, and cows will say yeccch. If the temperature rises too high, caramelized silage will form: cows love it, but it is not as nutritious as lactic acid silage. Most dairy farmers don't know much about the chemistry, but they generally know how to do it right.

Old-fashioned wooden silos are most often loaded and unloaded from the top. This means nothing can be added once the silage is made until all of it has been fed out. The new steel and fiber glass silos empty automatically from the bottom, so new crops can continually be added at the top. This allows higher production of feed per dollar invested in a silo and is just one more way the big farmer has the edge over his little cousin. The big man can push a button, and augers, conveyers, and robot dumping wagons will feed silage to a barnful of cows.

The little guy has to climb the silo, throw the day's

supply down to a loading bay, load it by the wheelbarrow, and dump it by hand in front of each cow. The little guy's cows pretty consistently produce a few thousand more pounds of milk each year than the big guy's cows, as a result of the individual attention, but that is nowhere near enough of an edge to give most little guys much of a future.

Speaking of little guys, old Solon Robinson, speaking from the year 1860, has the last word on corn: "It enters into the food of all classes of people, either as bread or meat, so that it may be said that it is as much a universal food crop with us as rice is in India. It is more important than rice, for it produces a higher order of civilization."

Politics of Country Living

For the urbanite who moves to the country, the new setting offers—or seems to for a time—the possibility of an existence more devoted to "essentials." But in this doom decade of our tragic kingdom, who even dares say what is essential? Where once gardening was obviously an industrious thing to do, and building-your-own-house was top-notch, nothing is unequivocally nifty anymore.

Our vision of the world insures that. We know too much about the relationship between our own actions and the ugly plight of most other citizens of the globe. And we know too much about that relentless flow of desecratingly ugly resort camps, snowmobile parks, ski resorts, and grotesque commercial fry-houses which will surely ooze through the future of these no longer sheltered hills.

A few years ago, such truths did not impinge on dreamers' visions of rural tranquility. Before the "country living movement" had taken hold, before the public imagination was titillated by the rambling monologues of Ray Mungo, the artistically brilliant lore of Alicia Bay Laurel, the staunch nobility of Scott Nearing, there seemed to many young people a very real conflict between "escaping" to the country and participating in some politically active urban life, intended to make the world a fit place to live.

Now the conflict seems less crucial. Perhaps more people are coming to feel that (a) there's no escaping no matter where you move, and (b) perhaps the life of the middle-class city activist isn't all that effective or rewarding. I suppose a few people are still battling with such considerations. My college-age friends thought it quaint that I even asked whether the activism-retreat issue still gets debated on campus. I confess to being sure, for many years, that "the good life" was wanting in altruism, reeked of self-indulgence, and carried on, at least by neglect, an age-old oppressive social order which we whippersnappers had unveiled for the first time. Well, that's over.

As for the revolution back where I saw it last, I hear it still goes on. I believe General Giap's axiom of revolutionary strategy: Convert whom you can, and neutralize whom you can't convert. But it is counterrevolutionary strategy as well—it is anybody's strategy—and has in fact served corporate interests in creating the current maleable and ineffectual U.S. body politic.

While the liberal reformers (who keep John Public believing that the system only wants perfecting) are building awareness of the limited interests now served by U.S. business practices, the most committed echelons of radicals ironically have failed to associate their own programs with the self-same diagnosis. By now everyone has gotten the we-are-serious-and—we-mean-business message of radicals. But news of radicals' rationales for meaning business, and of radicals' programs for reform, has not only failed to reach the people but has fostered the illusion in the mind of the public that revolutionaries are in fact merely demented and evil.

So the situation created during the late sixties by the growing corps of revolutionary converts (and by their straight-press publicists) seems very much contrary to revolutionary goals. As things stand, the public feels neutral not to revolutionary ideas but to the powers that be, and it permits these powers to continue a structure which could stand considerable change.

For a long time I held on to the faithful attitude that "there absolutely has to be a way somewhere to make things turn out for the best." But perhaps that is not the case, try as anyone might, with the project of political education in the 1970's. Myself, I reached the breaking point early in 1969, spent the next year feeling like a creep for leaving the fray, and then went about my business.

Of course I'm sure I'm not doing the most good I could be doing for other people. But I don't so much have the proprietary view of "people out there" as possible patrons of my services—that one not very oppressed must be a full-time doer of good. What little I know I am happy to share, but I no longer have earth shaking ministrations to purvey. You wanna know about rutabagas, I'll tell you about rutabagas. You wanna know about how to make a correct revolution? Me too.

My move from city politics to rural subsistence farming is anything but atypical. Living in the country has replaced radical political change as one of the more palatable end visions for people in our troubled society.

189

Not many years ago the plain dirt farmer was the stock stuff of jokes calling him foolish and naïve. Today, the same farmer is sought as a knowing guru, holder of ancient secrets of life, exemplar of a dying American tradition which once expressed some of the greater virtues of our national character.

But anyone who moves to the farm looking to retrieve what America has cast aside will suffer sure disappointment. Things are falling apart out here too. In the sticks the symptoms may lag ten or a dozen years behind the forthright urban expressions of strain, but they are discernible. Troubles do not take the form of holocaust here.

The trouble is more manifest in the numbness of the thousands of victimized young people who grew up on farms and, having been turned away from that life, live instead with TV, discount stores, and an ethos crackling with the mystique of dirty sex and violent punishment, daringly expensive playthings, and the universal veneer of middle class grace, unwittingly learned from the good-natured and hollow folks who populate the TV world. TV defoliates green old ways of life; it superimposes a stylishly dumbfounded passivity, a reluctance to make independent judgments, upon the lives of a nation of mill workers, salesmen, merchants, schoolchildren, executives, bedridden grandmothers—all with great impartiality.

As for the discount stores, they stand on the edge of town as monuments to the death of integrity. Customers in those horrifying acre-large trash yards are privileged to buy what amount to models of real things—tools that are shaped the same as real tools sold down the street that work, pants that look the same on the rack as pants sold down the street to be worn. Not only do merchandisers take advantage of a public conditioned to be acquiescent if not undiscriminating, their cheap selection of staple items and low labor cost per sale take customers away from the more responsible small merchants. When no one buys light bulbs, rope, paintbrushes, and gas cans at the hardware store, how can the store survive to supply us with ice tongs, galvanized double-headed nails, and drive-belt clamps? Of course only outlandish diehards need things like that anyway.

If one can overlook the dying out of locally owned small shops where, up until now, personal relations between townspeople and merchants have kept everybody more or less honest, perhaps one can also overlook the complex musical chairs game played by realtors, lawyers, and town officials, who seem frequently to trade offices, at no time straying too far from the courthouse square coffee shop where they are slicing the pie again and again. They are protected, as are the other good citizens of the county seat, by an up-to-date police force neither amateur nor pleasant, equipped with attack dogs and riot weapons. And the cops no longer regard themselves primarily as neighbohood guardians of tranquility. Today they read *Police Chief* and similar national professional magazines and see themselves (even here) as members of a vast force of underpaid, constantly endangered public servants whose sacrifice on behalf of local tranquility is seldom repaid. Their dealings with the public demonstrate their feelings.

If the goal of the would-be rural refugee is to escape our disintegrating society, he might as well try moving immediately to the Faroe Islands, which probably won't have him. If he insists on staying home, his only hope is a cave and hermitage.

What about those of us, unwilling to be hermits, who

NUTS TO CRACK

come anyway, with eyes open? Can we hope to lead decent lives which we find pleasant and not too compromising?

The life we accept here involves a certain amount of artifice, almost as a given, before one even begins to solve the problems of daily living. We are outsiders with city educations and social know-how. We have money-making opportunities and, at the same time, styles of living inexpensively which set us apart from the townspeople and make us in their eyes a new breed of year-round summer people. Perhaps we are scorned as hippies, perhaps as "rich folks from Connecticut," perhaps we are praised as neighbors who "keep to themselves" and are "always friendly enough."

The townspeople, of course, have their own ranks of educated citizens. But they are seldom in evidence. If someone's child gets to the state college, to medical school, to law school or becomes a professor, he is not likely to come back to town except to visit mom or

192

occasionally to set up a practice. Certainly he's not about to get a Ph.D. and then take up subsistence farming, as more than one friend of mine here has done.

I am asked, on visits to the city, "Who is there for you to talk to up there?" Until this writing, I never questioned the implications of my answer: "There are plenty of people who have settled around here for the same reasons I have. And I have a few local friends also." In short, despite fantasies to the contrary, I am not much a part of the ongoing social or political life of the town of Clabberville, and I don't imagine I could be if I tried. Perhaps I am living where I have no business living.

I am not farming enough to call myself a farmer, and I am not doing any of the other things people around here see fit to do. I don't work in the mill, I don't teach in the school, I don't go to many football games, I don't watch TV often, I don't work for the government, I don't cut timber, I don't hunt, I don't snowmobile, I don't have an easy way with bar banter.

And, needless to say, I do many strange things which defy the comprehension of those of the townspeople who trouble to think about me at all. I post my land, I garden organically, I heat with wood when I could afford not to. I sit in the local coffee shop in Shelby Basin and read the *New York Times*, I receive strange packages, and strange-looking visitors from out of town, straight-looking ones in big cars, mysterious-looking long-haired ones driving into my neighbors' yards at midnight in an emerald green schoolbus, searching for our farm. I live "without visible means of support" because I work at a desk right at home; I don't hide the sins of my bachelorhood.

I get on extremely well with the old-timers who are bred by a culture more tolerant of "eccentricity" or independence of mind than the current culture. I respect the old fellow who knows how to shoe an ox ("You gotta tie him and knock him down first"), and he likes that. A few of the younger farmers in the same tradition also are actual friends. I am living in a society I have some affection for, but which has little connection with me. Most of my social life is with others living as I do.

Friends on communes are less affected by this relationship to the town than I am, living with only a few others. The constant brouhaha a dozen old friends stir up in the rush of daily life fills them with events and projects, and leaves them little disposition to reflect on their awkward town-gown relations and I suppose it's not of much interest to them.

As for me, I have learned more about classes, working and ruling, than ever I knew in my bad old lefty days. Although I'm not extremely involved in community affairs here, I'm nevertheless more solidly rooted than I ever was when I was "terribly involved" (as my mother used to put it when explaining me to friends). There is life in the hinterlands; not everything happens most meaningfully in the big city. I am happier and therefore do more that I will and less that I must than in my former existence, and I hope I'm kinder to other people.

CONCLUSION.

A Note on the Type

This book was set on the Linotype in Janson, a recutting made direct from type cast from matrices long thought to have been made by the Dutchman Anton Janson, who was a practicing type founder in Leipzig during the years 1668–87. However, it has been conclusively demonstrated that these types are actually the work of Nicholas Kis (1650–1702), a Hungarian, who most probably learned his trade from the master Dutch type founder Dirk Voskens. The type is an excellent example of the influential and sturdy Dutch types that prevailed in England up to the time William Caslon developed his own incomparable designs from them.

Composed, printed, and bound by The Colonial Press Inc., Clinton, Massachusetts.

Typography and binding design by Clint Anglin.

10288

917.4422 Kramer, Mark
K

      Mother Walter
      and the pig
      tragedy

DATE			
JAN 7 JAN 23			